To Ruth

With love from Mother & Dad

Xmas. 1953.

TOM STETSON

and the

Blue Devil

By

JOHN HENRY CUTLER

Illustrated by
URSULA KOERING

WHITMAN PUBLISHING COMPANY

RACINE, WISCONSIN

CONTENTS

CONTENTS *(Continued)*

LIST
OF
ILLUSTRATIONS

ILLUSTRATIONS *(Continued)*

ILLUSTRATIONS *(Continued)*

Tom Wondered What Lay Ahead of Him

TOM STETSON
and the
Blue Devil

CHAPTER ONE

THE BLACK RAINLESS CLOUD

Tom Stetson yawned as he rested his hands on the railing of the launch that was skimming the surface of the coffee-colored Amazon. He looked up into the tropical blue sky of Brazil and let his mind wander for a moment back to Duxbury Bay, where he had spent so many vacations until his Uncle Leo, who was a veteran missionary, had invited him to explore the backwaters of the mysterious Amazon. He thought of his high-school friends who would be diving from the float, riding surfboards, and casting for bass and mackerel from an outboard motorboat.

Tom stretched out his arms and took a deep breath of the warm, moist air. He could feel the beads of perspiration on his forehead. Everything was so calm and peaceful. Except for the gentle throbbing of the *Paloma's* Diesel engine, a silence that seemed almost ominous had settled on the swift-flowing river. Tom looked over the side and thought of some of the things his uncle had told him about this amazing waterway.

The Amazon had an average depth of one hundred twenty feet during the rainy season that began in November. The brown river was not quite so swollen now, he told himself as his eyes grew dim with imagining the exciting adventures that lay just ahead. It was the third week in June, and the river would gradually be losing its flood waters until it reached its lowest level at the end of October. He wished he could stay on with his uncle visiting the uncharted backlands of Brazil. He would be quarterbacking the high-school football team in October, but even football was tame stuff compared to the adventure which he never failed to find in the jungle of the Amazon.

He sank onto a canvas chair and rested his folded arms on the railing. Even when everything seemed so quiet, he thought, you might be on the brink of dangerous adventure. Right here, under the smooth surface of this river, which carried four times as much water as the Mississippi, there were electric eels and man-eating fish only six or seven inches long. The most dangerous fish in the world was not the killer whale or the tiger shark. It was this deadly little piranha with its razor-like teeth, a terrible monster that came up in schools when attracted by the scent of blood. Tom sat upright and shuddered at the thought of the damage these piranhas could do. They could devour a crocodile in a matter of seconds if there were enough of them!

Tom could feel his heart thumping in his chest as the *Paloma* churned its way up the muddy river. He rested his wondering gaze on the dark-green walls of the rolling jungle that stretched out endlessly on both sides of the Amazon. The jungle was easy to see, for here the river was only about two miles wide. Behind that high wall of green lurked gigantic snakes, some of them poisonous. There were literally hundreds of kinds of insects of every color, shape, and size. Again he shuddered when he remembered the close calls he, his uncle, and Manolo had had with the alligator bug, or lantern fly. One sting from that big insect meant almost instant death. He kept his eyes glued on the jungle, as if he were trying to see one of the wild jungle animals or an Indian stalking through it. All at once Tom felt the weight of the mystery and the strange fascination of this jungle that was for the most part unmapped.

He rose from the chair and paced back and forth on the narrow deck, his hands clasped behind him. His imagination was playing tricks on him. As he glanced up at the cloudless sky he fancied he saw the Blue Devil grinning fiendishly down at him. "Go

back home to Boston, little tenderfoot," the imagi-
nary fiend seemed to be saying. "Don't you know that
none of the explorers and oil engineers and missionaries who have invaded my green forest have ever returned to tell about it? Death to all white men who
dare to venture into my domain!"

Tom paused at the railing and raised his binoculars. Suddenly as he trained them on the rim of the
horizon he saw a curiously shaped black cloud rolling in from the distance. It was coming toward
him slowly, like a huge black serpent. That's how
things were here in wonderful Brazil. Tom absent-
mindedly reached down to stroke the fur of Ozzy,
his pet ocelot, which was brushing against the back
of his legs. The hot tropical sun would beat down
like mad and then zing! A dark gray curtain would
shut out its blazing light and it would rain bucket-
fuls. Then the blackness of the day would fade. The
rain would stop as abruptly as it had started, and
once again the burning sun would leave the soaked
jungle steaming. At such times the tops of the towering jungle trees would be wrapped in a sort of fog.

"Guess we'd better slip into our oilskins, Uncle
Leo," Tom said. "Looks as if another rainstorm is
on its way."

Leo Jason, the white-haired medical missionary
who had been living among the uncivilized Indians
in the backlands of the Amazon Basin for more than

twenty years, gave no sign that he had heard what Tom had said. He seemed miles away, completely lost in thought. Tom looked at him fondly for a moment, then went below for their raincoats.

Tom saw that Manolo, the young Indian boy, was still sound asleep on his bunk. It would be some time before he would fully recover from the cruel treatment he had received from the savage Pomora Indians, a tribe that used fierce harpy eagles to guard their captives. Their captives died a thousand torturous deaths before they were put in a cage with one of those dreadful lantern flies. Then they died a final death. One sting from a lantern fly, which the Indians themselves called an alligator bug, meant sudden coma to the weakened person and then death. Tom ran a handkerchief over his brow which was as damp from the thought of those treacherous lantern flies as from the humid air. If he never saw another of those flies it would be okay with him!

Everything about that adventure had been exciting. There was the system of vine cables that led from tree to tree and connected the tribal villages. Two such tribes were enemies at the time Tom, his uncle, and Manolo had come upon them. Spies from the villages had made their way quickly and silently hand over hand on the vine cables above the brush and rank growth of the jungle.

The day-by-day lives of these people, even the

foods they ate, were a source of interest to Tom. These people were not farmers. They grew no grains. For the most part their food was made up of the fish and meat and fruits and nuts that the jungle offered them. But they did, almost without exception, grow a patch of manioc, and this shrub took the place of wheat and all other grains. They cared for the plants and gathered their large roots when they were ready. The roots, as they were, were poisonous, but the women grated the raw roots and, in baskets made especially for the purpose, extracted the poisonous juice. The pulp was then dried and used as flour to make the large, flat loaves of bread.

Stories of this kind amazed Tom. He could listen for hours to the tales his uncle had to tell about these primitive people.

When he went topside, he saw that his uncle was still thinking hard about something. While waiting to catch his eye, Tom's thoughts returned to the Blue Devil, the mysterious Indian who, according to Uncle Leo, had sworn to avenge the cruel treatment he and his family had received at the hands of some Brazilian explorers more than fifteen years ago. It seemed that the Blue Devil had returned one afternoon from a jaguar-hunting expedition when he saw his whole family lying dead near a spring. He found out later from his captors what had happened. The Brazilian white men had poisoned the waters just before the

Indians had come to drink. While the Blue Devil lifted his arms to the sky and vowed vengeance, a number of Brazilians rushed at him and knocked him to the ground. They tied him up so tightly there were blue welts when the rope was removed.

Tom sat on the deck and leaned against the railing. He glanced over his shoulder at the black cloud that had come closer, but he decided not to disturb his uncle for a minute or two. He knew from past experience that the missionary had important things on his mind when he remained silent and thoughtful for so long a time. Besides, it would be ten or fifteen minutes, perhaps, before the rains came. Tom closed his eyes and let his mind drift back to the Blue Devil.

The Brazilian explorers had forced him to tell them where the lost oil well was—a well that had been dug by some American oil company and which had later been abandoned because every worker sent into the vicinity had been murdered by an unknown Indian tribe. Uncle Leo was almost certain that the Blue Devil belonged to this tribe. After the oil engineers had left, the jungle had reclaimed the oil well that had been dug, and not until the Brazilian explorers had forced the Blue Devil to lead them to the site, was its whereabouts again known. But the explorers made one fatal mistake. They postponed for too long the execution of the Blue Devil in order to learn all they could from him. And so one day it happened. While the explorers were sitting around, the Blue Devil sneaked into the cabin where they kept their guns and murdered them in cold blood. And since then, said Uncle Leo, the Blue Devil had one burning ambition. It was to kill every white person who invaded his private domain.

Tom crossed his legs and rubbed his cheek thoughtfully. Uncle Leo probably knew more about the Blue Devil than any other white man. But he had no real idea as to the tribe to which he belonged. Possibly the treacherous Bororos, who also tried to murder every white man they encountered. But Uncle Leo thought it was more likely that the Blue Devil was a member of the Motilon tribe, which, he said, was the most dangerous in the Amazonian jungle. The Motilon Indians were seldom captured, for they darted like invisible lightning through the jungle, attacking silently and when least expected. They used heavy bows and arrows made out of black palm, and their aim was deadly.

"Say, Uncle Leo!" The words shot out of Tom's mouth before he realized he might be disturbing the missionary's train of thought. "How does it happen this mysterious Indian character is called 'The Blue Devil'?"

The missionary, who had scarcely moved a muscle during the half-hour or so he had been handling the wheel, turned his head in Tom's direction. A worried look had stolen into his features, as if the mere sound of the name "Blue Devil" had reminded him of the risk they were taking in penetrating his domain.

"Well, Tom, I'll tell you." The missionary fumbled in his pocket for his pipe. "Somehow that scalawag got hold of a lot of blue ribbon. You know, the kind your mother sometimes uses to tie up a birthday or Christmas present." He paused as he rose to let Tom help him into his raincoat.

Tom shot a quick glance at the black cloud that was now really getting close as he pulled the canvas chair nearer to his uncle. "What would a murderous savage want with any blue ribbon, Uncle? Seems like a sissy thing for a—"

"Anything but sissified, Tom Stetson." The missionary tilted his head to watch the lazy spiral of smoke rise and disappear. "The Blue Devil doesn't use that pretty ribbon for tying up birthday presents. As I told you, he roams the jungle like an invisible phantom, leaving death and destruction behind him. I hate to say it, but he seems to have learned some of his cruel tricks from so-called civilized white men. For example, he learned the art of torture from those Brazilians who captured him after they had murdered all his family."

Tom shifted uneasily in his seat. "But I don't get

it, Uncle. What has the blue ribbon got to do with this business of torturing?"

"Plenty, Tom." The missionary looked straight into his nephew's eyes. "Just before he strikes, this Indian ties a ribbon on a twig or something near his victim. He is the cockiest Indian I ever heard of. He warns before he attacks, and he seldom slips up. He's a lone wolf, moreover, according to any evidence we have about him. He may live with a tribe, but he operates alone."

Tom suddenly realized his jaw had dropped while his uncle had been talking. He felt bewildered and frightened at the same time. If this wily Indian was so dangerous, why were they going right into his domain, into his back yard, you might say? But Tom knew why they were going, and in spite of the dangers involved, he was glad he was part of the expedition. Uncle Leo felt it was his mission to try to civilize the Blue Devil.

There was a look of admiration on Tom's face as he studied his uncle's weather-beaten face. Here was a man of peace who took whatever risk was necessary to try to bring a bit of friendliness to savages. His only weapons were good will, persuasion, and understanding. He never carried a gun or any other weapon. He left trinkets and utensils at an attraction post, and if the Indian tribesmen accepted these token gifts, he took the chance they were friendly and tried to contact them. Tom looked at the missionary again. He was on his way now to find a lawless fiend and try to make him a friend instead of a dreaded enemy, but you might guess from his unconcern that he was on his way to a country fair.

"You know, Tom, I was just wondering what life will be like in this jungle in another thousand years or so." The missionary rose and stretched. "Want to take the wheel for a while, my boy?" He glanced at his watch. "Three-thirty. We ought to reach the secret river in a couple of hours."

Tom ran a hurried look over the compass as he sank into the seat. He felt a warm glow of contentment sweeping over him. He was so lucky to have an uncle in such an interesting part of the world. And one who let him share his exciting life. But this time, Uncle Leo had tried to talk him out of spending the summer with him in Brazil, because of the unusual hazards of the mission. But Tom had pleaded to come, and he had finally got permission from his parents to do so. He whistled softly to himself after glancing at his uncle, who had the field glasses trained on the black cloud.

Making Christians out of wild Indians who had never seen white men before was only part of Uncle Leo's job, however. He also taught them hygiene and treated them when they were sick. But almost every day he was in the jungle, no matter what his mission, Uncle Leo was risking his life. As he had once said himself, "You never know, when you are in the jungle, what murderous eyes are watching you from behind the nearest tree, and what kind of monster will crash out of the thicket."

Tom saw that Uncle Leo was still intently regarding the odd-shaped black cloud. It wasn't one of those thunderheads that appeared almost every afternoon, Tom told himself. He shifted into a more comfortable position.

Even before he had come to Brazil, Tom had heard about the weird monsters that were supposed to live far back from the main course of the Amazon. This mighty stream, called the "King of Rivers," had more than eleven hundred tributaries, and most of the tributaries had little muddy streams of their own flowing into them. The tawny brown Amazon, full of eerie fish and armored creatures that looked like crocodiles, but were far more deadly, was different from the darker backland streams that were so acid and stagnant that it was impossible for fish to live in them. Think of it! They were so acid that even jungle life was impossible in them. Uncle Leo had laughed when he had asked if there were beasts like dinosaurs, which were holdovers from the Age of Reptiles, and whether there were really snakes that weighed five tons.

"That's supposed to be the kind of rubbish you

They Watched the Strange Black Cloud

read in the Sunday newspaper supplements, Tom,"
he had said. "But, of course," he had added, "there are
plenty of strange things that no white man has ever
seen, and in the most remote regions there could be
some of those ghoulish reptiles you read about."

Tom looked up dreamily to find that his uncle
was smiling at him.

"Tom, you were a million miles away," the missionary said. He tapped his pipe on the railing to
get rid of the ashes and put the pipe in his pocket.
"What's on your mind? Were you figuring out a
tricky new play for your high-school football team
next fall?" He ran his eyes over Tom's face, tanned
almost to a mahogany color. "With all this outdoor
life, you should round into good shape."

Tom put a piece of candy in his mouth and threw
the paper box over the side. "Remember what you
told me about this jungle, Uncle Leo?" He made a
sweeping movement with his arm without turning
his head. "You said a pilot could drop a china cup
from an airplane five miles up without breaking it.
You said the cup would land in the foliage and
never reach the ground."

The missionary sank to the deck and leaned back
against the railing. "That's about it, my boy. I
can remember when railroad ties were shipped here
from Australia to build the toy railroad, as we call
it, from Guajará Mirim on the Mamoré River to

Porto Velho on the Madeira River." Uncle Leo
waited until he caught his nephew's eye. "Just imagine, Tom—transporting railroad ties into the biggest forest in the world. Why? Because it was too
much trouble to cut logs a hundred yards from the
rivers because there were no roads over which they
could be carried." He crossed one knee over the
other and drummed on the deck with his hand. "Of
course, there was another reason, too."

Tom glanced at him curiously. Whenever his
uncle paused like this, something interesting was
sure to follow. "Yes, Uncle?"

"It was too expensive to ship in a sawmill and
to keep men working. We have a saying around
here that 'Fever claimed a human life for every rail
put down.'

"These jungles have fired the imagination of
many men. Groups of them, from time to time, have
searched for minerals and oil and fabulous fortunes,
but this country does not welcome intruders. Even
the airplane and modern science have not found a
way to make the land profitable and livable. The
rains, the forest, the animals and insect pests, and
above all, tropical fevers and disease have succeeded
in keeping the Amazon valley as it has been for
hundreds of years. Even today the world knows
little of this land."

Tom walked to the railing. "Say, Uncle, one of

my ambitions is to see that wonderful city called Manaos, which you said was about a thousand miles up the Amazon from Belem." He whistled his amazement. "Jumping greensticks, imagine a city where you can ride to the end of the line in a trolley and then go hunting for jaguars! A city with a big opera house that's just an arrow's shot from head-hunters, wow! When are we going to Manaos, Uncle?"

But the missionary wasn't listening. He was again studying the black cloud through the field glasses. "Hmmmmm. Very interesting, very interesting." He poked Tom in the ribs playfully. "In a few minutes you're going to see something you'll never forget. But let's see—oh, yes, you were asking about that trip to Manaos. It all depends on how we make out on this little jaunt, Thomas. But in any case, if we don't squeeze in a trip to Manaos this summer, we'll certainly make one next summer. That is," he added, "if the Lord is willing. I'm getting old, you know."

As Tom steadied the wheel he realized that he was learning many things that no books could teach him. In the diary he kept in his pocket he noted down all the breath-taking sights of Brazil.

What a lot of things he would have to tell his family and his classmates! He smiled as he thought of how astonished they would be at some of his stories. He knew they would probably think that some of them were simply tall tales. And he wouldn't really blame them. A year ago he would have thought many of the things he had seen this summer just couldn't be.

What a greenhorn, what a tenderfoot he had been when he first had come to this country, which is as large as the United States and Alaska combined! He remembered how his eyes had almost popped out of their sockets the first time he had seen caterpillars seven inches long and an inch in diameter, which grew into moths that sometimes measured fourteen inches from wing tip to wing tip!

Tom was about to address his uncle when he saw he was again lost in thought. He remembered how strange his stomach felt when Uncle Leo had told him some Amazon Indians ate boiled caterpillars, ants, and beetles. He pursed his lips and shook his head from side to side violently, as if to drive away the memory of those blasted ants more than an inch long. He had seen millions of them in one army of destruction, and he didn't ever want to see any more of them—and yet, in a way, he did, it was such an astonishing sight.

A quick look told Tom that the black cloud over-head was about to burst. He buttoned the top button of his oilskin. One night an army of tocandeira ants had eaten a pair of his uncle's heavy-duty shoes, leaving the nails in a pattern shaped like the soles of the shoes. There had been something ghostly about the business. He didn't particularly want to tangle with any of those termites that were four inches long, either, but he knew that before this summer was over, he'd see a lot more things he didn't want to see. Again he shifted nervously in his seat. The thoughts that were seeping into his mind! He realized all at once that his uncle was talking to him.

"The word jungle comes from a Hindu word that means 'waste ground,' and in one sense that's just what this jungle is—'waste ground.' But someday, my boy, things will be different. Just as there are buried cities and vanished civilizations under the green carpet of the jungle, the day will surely come when there will be bustling cities, heavy traffic, athletic stadiums, and skyscrapers where wild tapirs and other jungle beasts now roam."

Tom's eyes were popping. He saw that the usual twinkle was missing from Uncle Leo's eyes. He was dead serious! "Did you say skyscrapers, Uncle?"

The missionary went on as if he had not heard. "This jungle is for the most part uninhabited, but it could hold two or three—maybe four or five —hundred million people without too much crowding." He sank wearily to the deck, leaned back against the railing and hunched up his knees. "This jungle is somewhat like Johannesburg was about sixty years ago."

"Why, Uncle!" Tom looked to see if his uncle was joking. "Johannesburg is the most modern city in South Africa, Uncle Leo. If I remember my geography correctly, it has a population of half a million, broad avenues, parks—"

"And up-to-date hotels, skyscrapers, churches, schools, and hospitals," broke in the missionary. "Its railroad station alone cost three million dollars. But sixty years ago—about the time I was born, I'd say —the inhabitants were primitive men and wild animals." He pulled his pipe out of his pocket and waved it in the direction of the jungle wall, which was getting closer. "Of course, we know far less about that country in there than the world knew about the jungles of Africa sixty years ago."

Tom unbuttoned his raincoat. "I can't figure out why it isn't getting cooler, Uncle. It usually does when a storm lowers."

The missionary was smiling. "I'll take the wheel now, Thomas. Take a peek through your binoculars and you'll understand why it isn't getting cooler. That's no storm cloud up there."

Tom had a numb feeling as he took the field glasses. He raised them and kept them focused on the tremendous black cloud, now smack overhead. He gasped at the sight of the advancing cloud. "I'll say that's no storm cloud up there, Uncle!" Tom's voice trailed off and he gazed spellbound at one of the most breath-taking sights in his young life. It was a beautifully colored ribbon, a tangle of reds, greens, and gleaming yellows and every other shade of color you could mention. Millions of butterflies were migrating!

CHAPTER TWO

THE SECRET RIVER

For a moment Tom was too stunned to say a word. He kept his eyes glued on the column that stretched back for what seemed miles. He had seen Brazilian butterflies before, huge butterflies with a wing-spread of a foot. But never before had he seen, and never before had he heard of, so many of them at once.

When the butterflies had poured out of the sun temple in the Pomora village, forming what had looked like a mammoth bandanna, he had taken colored pictures of the wonderful spectacle. But for every butterfly there had been in that swarm, there were thousands in this one.

"Oh, boy!" Tom murmured. "I wish they were lower so I could take some pictures." He turned away for a moment to find his uncle intently studying the column that was now almost directly over the bow of the *Paloma*. "How many would you say there are up there, Uncle?"

Even the usually placid missionary seemed impressed by the sight. "It's hard to say, Tom." He walked to the hatchway. "Manolo, can you come up

33

for a minute?"

Tom shook his head unbelievingly as he watched the snaky, colored ribbon advance overhead. What gorgeous creatures they were, with their colored dots and markings that no artist could ever hope to imitate! He wondered how so many of them, so closely banked together, could move along so smoothly and gracefully without bumping into one another. He drew in his breath sharply. There were so many of them they were blotting out the sun. Tom whirled around at the sound of footsteps.

"Hi, Manolo. Isn't that terrific up there?"

Manolo, who was in his early teens like Tom, rarely smiled, and almost never looked surprised. He was wearing the same kind of outfit as Tom, a khaki short-sleeved shirt, khaki shorts, and blue sneakers. His tropical helmet was not on at the moment.

As Manolo looked through the binoculars that Tom handed him, Tom wondered once again about the mystery that shrouded the little Indian boy's origin. All Tom knew about Manolo was that his uncle had adopted him eleven years ago when the Indian was a skinny, undernourished youngster of three or four. Uncle Leo had found the sad-faced child in an abandoned settlement not far from the headwaters of the dark Xingu River, where head-hunters and other wild savages roamed, hunting for animals and white men. Manolo, Tom knew, belonged to one of the primitive tribes haunting the rain-soaked forest in that unmapped region, but Uncle Leo had never been able to find out which one, as hard as he had tried. For when found curled up in a dirty hammock, Manolo could speak only a few words, and they were in an Indian dialect unfamiliar to Uncle Leo.

Tom saw the look of interest that had crept into Manolo's usually impassive bronze features as he trained the glasses on the cloud of butterflies. Manolo returned the binoculars to Tom. "Many more than we see in many moons," he said gravely. "They fly two week without rest. Cover sometime one, sometime two thousand mile."

The missionary was guiding the *Paloma* toward the shore.

"Poor critters," he said, glancing upward. "Sometimes a gust of wind drives them out to sea and they drown by the million." He took off his tropical helmet and mopped the perspiration from his forehead. "It's hard for us humans to comprehend the vast numbers of insects. I can't see well enough to tell what kind of butterflies are up there, but one swarm of 'Painted Ladies' I saw years ago numbered about three billion, according to a naturalist who was with me at the time. As far as I know, no other species of butterfly goes on such extended trips or in such vast numbers." He looked up again. "That column is approximately half a mile wide, a quarter of a mile deep and five or six miles long. For a rough guess, I'd say there were ten to fifteen million of them, but I could be several millions off one way or the other."

Tom was pacing the deck nervously. "Gosh, Uncle, if these confounded insects keep multiplying, maybe they'll take over the earth some day." He lowered his glasses. "My arms are aching from holding these binoculars, but it sure was worth it."

"I've seen places where insects have already taken over, Tom." The medical missionary smiled at Manolo as the sober-eyed young Indian went below. "Ants often drive settlers out of their diggings. Once in Paraguay I saw a swarm of locusts that covered over a hundred square miles of sky. Sometimes they eat everything in their path. A swarm of insects that may be as long as fifty miles, and be ten miles wide and three or four miles deep, can do terrible damage. They eat crops and are in turn eaten by some other creature."

There was a puzzled look on Tom's face. "It would take an awful lot of creatures to eat a fifty-mile column of insects, wouldn't it, Uncle?"

"Sure would, Tom."

"I suppose the dampness and the heat give this country its full share of insects," Tom offered, thinking back to some of his lessons in natural science he had had in school.

"Yes, Brazil has more than its share of insects," Uncle Leo said and then added, "some are good and some only add to the complicated life here in the jungle.

"There is a story told of how an early British scientist reported that he could find about seven hundred species of butterflies within an hour's walk of the place where he was staying. In Europe, it is said, there are but something like three hundred species. These insects, of course, add to the beauty of the country, but there are the others—mosquitoes and piums—"

"Oh, yes, I've made their acquaintance," Tom said, shivering as he thought of the swarms of humming, biting insects he had fought.

"Yes, they add no beauty to the landscape nor are they of any good that I can see. They add only to the discomfort of living here. Termites, too—and then the spiders. Did you know, Tom, that there is one spider that feeds on small birds? It has a body about two inches long and the outstretched legs measure seven inches."

"Oh, boy!" Tom exclaimed. "That really is a spider! I'm not too anxious to meet up with one of those."

"Well, Nature has also provided a number of birds and animals and reptiles that live on these insects. It is really a wonderful thing how the balance of life is kept throughout the natural world," Uncle Leo added. The *Paloma* nosed in the direction of a heavy overhang of jumbled foliage. "The three million bats that live in the Carlsbad Caverns in New Mexico eat tons of insects every night."

Tom continued his nervous pacing of the deck. "Well, Uncle Leo," he remarked, grinning, "if the insects eat all the crops and the bats eat all the insects, maybe we'll have to get used to eating roast bats."

"In the tropics," the missionary said slowly, "it is sometimes necessary to eat strange things, Tom. But I hope we'll never have to stave off starvation by eating the kind of bats we have down here."

Tom sat on the railing and folded his arms. "You mean that even the bats are different, Uncle?"

The missionary was guiding the *Paloma* toward a narrow channel. "There are several different kinds down here, Tom. There's the leaf-nosed bat which is large, but pretty harmless. I have seen two species of white bats, and I understand there are white bats in Central America, also. But the bad ones I'm referring to are those blood-sucking vampire bats which, if they get the chance, will suck the blood of both animals and men. They are fiendishly clever at finding the right artery or blood vessel in a sleeping person."

The Paloma Nosed Into the Channel

"Don't say any more, Uncle. Or I'll never dare take a nap in the jungle again." Tom threw a dog biscuit to Ozzy, the pet ocelot, which was stretching its forepaws on the deck.

"Well, Tom, it's always a good idea to be prepared for the worst. You never know when you're in the jungle whether some enemy may cut you off, so when the food supply runs out, it's well to know which plants are edible and which ones are dangerous to touch."

"Like those man-eating plants you once told me about, Uncle?" Ozzy was purring contentedly as Tom stroked his fur.

"Righto, Tom. There are several varieties of plants that ensnare insects even in the United States. One is the Venus's-flytrap which scientists say can actually develop indigestion if it devours too many insects. At least it drops anything it can't digest. Then there is the sundew which attracts insects with the tiny drops of sticky fluid on the hairs of its leaves. When the insect lights, the hairs ensnare it. The plant digests the parts it can eat, then opens the hairs and the hard parts of the insect fall away. There is also the pitcher plant found in the United States. Its leaves are roughly cup-shaped and are partly filled with a carrion-smelling liquid. When an insect comes to investigate the liquid, tiny hairs on the lip of the cup keep it from finding its way out. You see, the hairs all point downward and the insect cannot crawl up over them.

"But here around the Amazon there are plants that can capture animals. I have never seen one myself, but a missionary friend of mine told me he saw a man-eating tree, a towering growth that he said sometimes had a spread of twelve feet. The leaves are studded with claw-like thorns, and when man or animal comes within clutching range, the leaves close in on them and hold their grip until the flesh has been digested. Generally it takes two or three days, I learned. And then—this is a scary thought, too, Tom—the leaves unfurl and shed the remnants, that is, the bones."

"Let's talk about something more cheerful, Uncle. Jeekers, but that passageway we're heading for is narrow. What are some of the life-saving plants you hinted at, in case I ever find myself marooned with an empty water canteen?"

The missionary was manipulating the wheel carefully to keep from hitting a thick wall of vegetation on the starboard side. "One is the bark of a vine that grows wild in these jungles around here. The Indians make a drink called yocco out of it. It's really a grand drink when you feel weary. It—"

"You mean you've had some of it, Uncle?"

"Yes, two or three times, when I had no other

nourishment. On one of my trips near the Xingu River I lived for five days on nothing but yocco and felt no ill effects afterward. The bark of this vine has a high concentration of caffeine in it, which explains why it gives you such a lift. And it kills your appetite, too, so maybe doctors back home may some day be prescribing it for their overweight patients. It gives you muscular stimulation at the same time it makes you forget about your hunger. Maybe we'll find the vine bark somewhere in here. We may also find some of those amazing agricultural ants, which we can fry in a pinch."

Tom was perched over the bow of the *Paloma* as his uncle piloted it toward what now seemed like a tunnel. "I think I read something about farming ants, Uncle Leo. Is that what you mean?"

"Right again. They appear to cultivate patches of wild rice and other forms of food and keep out all the weeds until the crop ripens. Then they climb the stalks, harvest the grain, and carry it away for storage purposes in their underground granaries. At least this is the story some men tell. Some scientists, however, have claimed to disprove this theory."

Tom scarcely heard the last few words. He could feel his heart pounding like a triphammer. The launch was pushing its way gently with a rustling sound through a leafy wall that yielded passage and then closed behind them, as if covering their retreat into the jungle stream. It was almost dark. Suddenly Tom realized where they were!

"So this is the secret river leading to the domain of the Blue Devil, Uncle Leo?"

CHAPTER THREE

A RIVER MONSTER

The *Paloma* skimmed through the semi-darkness of the leafy tunnel, and now for the first time Tom felt the full mystery of his wild surroundings. It seemed so strange to be cruising into the ragged edge of nowhere on the trail of a mysterious Indian tribe that was led by a fiend known only as the Blue Devil. Tom was about to say something when he noticed his uncle was intent on guiding the launch through the narrow channel. At this point the secret river was narrow, and the missionary was being unusually cautious to keep from running aground.

"You never know what we may run into when we cruise into an unmapped stream like this, Tom," the missionary said. He was huddled over the wheel as he spoke. "During the high-water season even some ocean steamers can navigate many of these tributaries, which are much deeper than you'd imagine. But at other times even a small boat like ours may suddenly find itself on the edge of a waterfall. Want to go below to see if Manolo is feeling strong enough to come topside? We may need his advice before we get much farther."

It was still quite dark, and Tom's first impulse was to turn on his flashlight as he moved toward the hatchway. But he remembered his uncle's warning in time—be careful about revealing your position when you are in unfamiliar territory. He also remembered the fascinating stories about the gourds with holes punched into them. There were Indians roaming the Amazon jungle who filled these gourds with fireflies and used them as crude lamps!

He took care to make as little noise as possible as he went below.

In some parts of the tropics even civilized women wore large fireflies in their hair as ornaments. Imagine wearing live bugs instead of jewelry, pinning fireflies in your hair and on your clothes to make yourself look beautiful! It was a strange thought.

"Are you awake, Manolo?" Tom leaned over the bunk and saw the young Indian's wan smile. He waited while Manolo slowly drew himself up into a sitting position. It wouldn't be long before his loyal little friend would be himself again. He was regaining his strength slowly, but he was a rugged fellow when he was in good condition.

Without a word Manolo trailed Tom topside. The *Paloma* was still purring its way through the leafy tunnel as Tom slumped onto the deck and watched the little Indian take in the situation. He was getting impatient, now. He wished they'd get to the end of this confounded secret tunnel.

His imagination cut loose again. He wondered whether there were any ruined towers on high hills around this neck of the woods. Could there be towers like those amazing ones perched up in the Andes Mountains in Peru, which his uncle said he had once seen? The missionary had come on two such towers one afternoon when he wandered from the regular mountain trail. He said they looked as if they were hundreds of years old. There were iron hooks fastened to each tower so that a gigantic net could be stretched between them. Tom remembered how shocked he had been when his uncle told him why the primitive Indians had hung the net in this odd place. It was a net to catch the sun, believe it or not! The Incas who had lived in Peru for so many hundreds of years—perhaps thousands of years— were sun-worshipers, and their sun temples were really something to see, Uncle Leo often said. Tom wondered whether the Blue Devil worshiped the moon or the sun.

Tom remembered that the Pomora tribe had been sun-worshipers. He thought of the butter-flies that those Indians had kept in their sun temple. What a wonderful sight that colored stream of insects had made as they flew from the building! It must have been a tremendous job to col-

lect those thousands of butterflies. Tom wondered
if perhaps the Indians had waited for such a mi-
gration as they had just seen and he had mis-
taken for a cloud. If they did, they might then
have caught hundreds of them with a net. That
was a question he must remember to ask Uncle
Leo.

"Hear that snarling sound?" the missionary said
softly without the slightest trace of emotion. He almost seemed to be sniffing the air, as if to tell something about the wild surroundings.

"Jaguar kitten." Manolo said it with a tone of
quiet authority. Tom always marveled at his jungle
lore. He was a wonderful pal to have around when
you were lost in the wilderness. "In tree," he added.

Tom shifted uneasily and rested his elbow on the
railing. "Let's hope it doesn't decide to pounce on
us." He wished something would happen to break
the suspense, yet he somehow dreaded the prospect.
His breathing was hurried now, and he found himself clasping and unclasping his hands. It was hard
to say what might happen in this dark jungle. Here
the stream was wider, but it still wound around and
around. In the shadowy light it looked almost as
black as coal. Tom started at the sound of something
that plumped onto the deck. He rested his hands on
his knees and bent over to study the object. It looked
like a branch about six inches long. Had somebody

thrown it or had it simply fallen from the canopy of foliage all around them? He stooped down to pick it up.

Manolo had whirled at the sound, as slight as it had been, and before Tom's outstretched fingers could touch the branch, he kicked it over the side. He looked at Tom apologetically. "Matacaballo," he said softly. "Full of much danger."

Tom could feel his lips trembling. "Mata . . . caballo . . ." he murmured unbelievingly. "So that's what one of those critters looks like?" He backed slowly toward the railing and sat down on it, resting his hands on his knees. He knew that a matacaballo, or "horse-killer," looked like a gray, dry branch that had been broken off at one end; he also knew that this was one of those devilishly clever tricks of jungle camouflage. This creature was a living animal, and although it didn't seem to have any means of locomotion, this insect could jump. Uncle Leo had once mentioned that horses often got into trouble by eating them, and that was the reason the natives of the Amazonian Basin called them matacaballos, or horse-killers. The insect had two thin legs on both sides, and if closely observed, the missionary had said, it could be seen moving slightly near its tail. If necessary, it could move forward with the speed of a torpedo being launched from the deck of a PT boat.

"Well, here we are, fellows," the medical missionary said as the *Paloma* suddenly poked its prow out from beneath the shadowy foliage into the dazzling sunlight. "And what happens next is your guess." He studied the thick jungle that now was closing in on them on all sides as he spoke. "South American Indians often choose this kind of country to settle in. And there's more than one reason for it. They like to be near the edges of a river basin, and they also like some high land so they can keep an eagle eye on what's going on below them. From here on in, mates, we're back in the Stone Age. And just bear in mind every minute that we can't be too careful."

Tom, who had jumped to his feet the moment they had left the tunnel, had the impression that they had just emerged from an underground river. Here they were, in the world's last great wilderness —the farthest he had ever been from home and civilization. He rested his hands on his hips and glanced around curiously. All around them were more than four million square miles of trackless jungle, full of wild beasts and humans who were far more dangerous than the beasts. Tom was sure this wilderness was inhabited. He knew his uncle would never waste any valuable time plowing into this back country if he wasn't reasonably certain of finding Indians in it. He blinked into the sun as his eyes, partly shaded by his tropical helmet, got used to the bright light.

"Everything looks so calm and peaceful you'd think we were the only living creatures around," he said. He shaded his eyes from the glare of the tropical sun and grinned at his uncle. "But I expect to run into a dinosaur or a sea serpent any minute. I suppose it's about time I got used to hearing all your stories about ferocious beetles six inches long, oysters that weigh seventeen pounds and whales that have eyes as big as grapefruit."

The missionary puffed on his pipe and smiled. "I don't remember telling you anything about giant oysters. I think you've been reading those Sunday supplements again, Tom."

Tom ran his fingers through his blond hair and grinned. "Well, Uncle Leo, if I'm going to be an explorer, I figure it's best that I read all I can about the things I'm apt to run into while cruising around. I remember reading last winter about a five-hundred-pound man-eating clam that is found down in French Malaya." He shuddered at the thought. "Jeekers, it gives me the creeps just to think of those monsters." He looked straight into his uncle's eyes. "Why, Uncle, I read that sometimes the natives down there are trapped and eaten by them. Ugh! Just imagine clams three feet long." He slumped onto the deck and hunched up his knees.

"I've never run into anything like that, Tom, but if I ever found myself in the water I'd take my chances with an oversized clam before I'd want to tangle with a school of piranhas. Mere size doesn't always mean very much. Clams, for example, are slow-moving. And those huge tortoises they have on the Galapagos Islands—some of them used to weigh around five hundred pounds, too, by the way, before they were slaughtered by wild dogs and men who hunted them and their eggs for oil—are really quite harmless. A boy could ride safely on their backs."

"Tom look like coconut hit him." Manolo smiled.

"Whew!" Tom shook his head and pursed his lips. Tortoises that weigh a quarter of a ton, wow! The world was sure full of wonders. How could anyone ever be bored? "Say, Uncle, is it true that tortoises sometimes live to be two or three hundred years old?"

The missionary stifled a yawn and shifted in his seat. "I doubt it, my boy. Some may, just as an Englishman named Thomas Parr lived to the ripe age of one hundred and fifty-two. Maybe some tortoises live two or three hundred years, but it would be unusual if they did."

Tom stretched out his arms and yawned. A short distance from the *Paloma* he could see a fish skimming over the surface of the dark brown water. He wondered whether it was being chased by some larger fish. But even as he watched his eyes closed and he felt himself drifting off to sleep.

"Quick, Tom!" The missionary was pointing excitedly to something. "About fifty yards astern! There's a big fish of some kind thrashing around on the surface!"

Tom scrambled to his feet and turned wide-eyed in the direction his uncle was pointing. He gasped at the sight of a huge monster that was churning through the dirty water, diving and surfacing at irregular intervals. He scarcely noticed that the missionary had changed course so he could circle around the monstrous fish. "What—what is it, Uncle Leo?" he asked.

The missionary, who usually took everything so calmly, was excited now. He waited for the creature to resurface before he spoke. "Get your camera, quick, Tom!" he said. "I believe it's some species of sea turtle."

Tom rushed below for the camera and a moment later was taking a picture of the creature that was still thrashing about wildly. He was too overcome to say anything, and finally, when the monster dived under the water for the last time, he sank on a deck chair, limp with excitement.

The missionary was shaking his head in disbelief as he swung the launch back onto the course they were following. "Why, you'd almost think we were nearing the age of reptiles," he said. "I couldn't get

"It Looks Like a Monster!"

a good look at that creature, but from what I saw of it I'd almost swear it was a leathery turtle. Odd. We were just talking about tortoises." He mopped his perspiring forehead and revved up the motor. "That specimen measured a good six feet from its snout to the tip of its tail."

"Take me out, coach, I've had enough," Tom said, leaning back in his chair with his legs spread wide. "At first I thought we were seeing one of those sea serpents sailors are always supposed to be seeing. A leathery turtle did you say?"

"It just couldn't be, Tom, but it must be a cousin of the leathery turtle. My boy, you'll never see another creature like that one in a month of Sundays. And want to know something?"

Tom's eyes were popping. He knew from his uncle's expression that something exciting was coming.

"The reason that monster was thrashing around like that is that it was being chased or attacked by some bigger or fiercer fish."

Tom, too excited to say a word, waited for him to continue.

"But I don't know what kind of fish down in a jungle stream could attack a creature that seemed to have as much armor as a leathery turtle."

"What about piranhas, Uncle?"

"Possibly, if that creature had soft underpinning. But since he managed to escape whatever was pursuing him, it couldn't have been piranhas, come to think of it. You don't get out of range of their sharp teeth so easily. I'm positive there are no tiger sharks or swordfish types down here, because they, like any types of leathery turtles I ever heard of, are salt-water fish."

"Maybe we're really coming into the land of dino-saurs, Uncle Leo." Tom leaned over the side and watched for any further trace of the monster, which had left ripples on the surface that were now lapping the shore. "Can swordfish get the better of leathery turtles?"

"Oh, yes indeed, my boy." The missionary shaded his eyes and scanned the shoreline. "They've been known to thrust through twenty-seven inches of solid wood, you know, so they would have no qualms about attacking a sea turtle, in spite of its tough hide. The only other leathery sea turtle I ever saw had powerful forelimbs with a stretch of about ten feet. And you'd never be able to guess where I saw it."

Tom paced back and forth restlessly, his hands on his hips. "I don't know where you saw it, Uncle, but if I ever see one I hope it's in an aquarium. That thing we just saw looked a bit unfriendly as far as I'm concerned."

"I saw the first one beached at low tide in Glouces-ter Harbor, of all places. If memory serves, it tipped the scales at slightly more than a thousand pounds, which is by no means unusual for a sea turtle." He looked searchingly at Tom while he tamped down the tobacco in his pipe. "I know what you're thinking. What was a leathery sea turtle doing around Gloucester, right?"

"Right. All we get around Duxbury are big blackfish and now and then a whale." Tom continued pacing the deck as he nodded. "That's exactly what I was thinking. Didn't you once tell me that sea turtles inhabited tropical waters?"

"I certainly did. Tropical or semi-tropical waters of both hemispheres." He turned to look back toward the spot where they had seen the monster. "But now and then they are found shored on Long Island or Massachusetts, especially after violent nor'easters." He rested his arm on Tom's shoulder when his nephew paused near him. "They look fierce, but in cold water they flounder around and can easily be harpooned or battered to death. They never come ashore, by the way, except to deposit their eggs."

"That's okay with me." Tom grinned as he sat down. He had no desire to come face to face with one of the huge beasts. Then his face clouded. As he combed the jungle with his field glasses, he felt the thrill of dangerous adventure. "This is it," he said to himself. Here were the haunts of Indians who hated white men, very likely.

Manolo was pointing. "More butterflies," he said.

Tom could see some of them fluttering a short distance from the *Paloma*. There was an offshore wind, and it was strong enough to carry these beautiful creatures to their doom. They would struggle to return until they dropped from sheer exhaustion. Almost every animal would fight fiercely to live. His thoughts drifted to the only animal he knew of that seemed to commit suicide—the lemming. He had read that every now and then millions of these rat-like creatures rush down from the mountains of Norway and plunge into the sea, where they drown. But these poor butterflies were being blown to their doom, the way flocks of birds often were.

Tom mopped his dripping brow. The torrid sun was really beating down. He went below and returned a moment later with glasses of cold papaya juice for all of them. "I think we could stand a cool drink," he said. "I know I could."

The missionary's face lighted up. "Thanks, Tom. You look puzzled. What's on your mind?"

"Oh, nothing much, Uncle. I was just wondering about those lost mountains of Brazil." His glance rested on Manolo, who was taking in the surrounding territory through his narrowed eyes. "Maybe we'll stumble on those lost gold mines you used to talk about."

"I doubt it, Tom." The missionary was studying both sides of the river, which was more than a hundred yards wide at this point. "But I must admit that there is an official document that says there is, somewhere in this jungle, a large city built of stone blocks." He looked up at Tom. "If we ever catch the Blue Devil, I have an idea that he will know something about that lost city."

CHAPTER FOUR

THE MYSTERIOUS PIER

Tom felt his jaw sagging. "You don't expect to capture this Blue Devil fiend, do you, Uncle?"

The missionary shook his head as he steadied the wheel. "Well, not exactly. But we may get a chance to talk to him, you know. Strange as it may be, he speaks pretty good English, too, I have heard."

Tom shifted restlessly in his seat and crossed his legs. "Maybe that's another reason he wants to keep white men out of his private domain. Maybe he is guarding the lost city."

The missionary shrugged. "Anything is possible down here, my boy. Sometimes I wish I could live long enough to solve all the mysteries buried in this green jungle. That city we are talking about, for example. I don't know whether I've ever told you and Manolo that the official document I mentioned is now in the royal public library in Rio de Janeiro."

"You better brief me on that lost city, in case I ever find it, Uncle." Tom grinned. "It would be awful if I should come across it and not recognize it." He still felt drowsy in the late afternoon heat, and he was tempted to stretch out on the deck and close his eyes. But curiosity was now getting the better of his fatigue. He preferred to see and hear everything that was going on.

"The history of Brazil is filled with stories of strange happenings," Uncle Leo began. "This country was discovered back in 1499 by a companion of Columbus. He took possession in the name of Spain but did not make a settlement of any kind. He did, however, take home with him specimens of drugs, gems, and brazilwood—products that were native to this land. But Spain at this time was busy elsewhere in the world and nothing very much was done to settle the country.

"Then in 1500 the Portuguese king appointed Pedro Cabral to follow the course of Vasco de Gama. He was driven so far from his course that he, by mistake, reached Brazil. He arrived on Good Friday and with the natives watching celebrated the Easter Mass on shore. In memory of his discovery he erected a stone cross. But still no settlement was made.

"For thirty years little attention was paid to the discovery of this really valuable country. Finally the Portuguese king, probably feeling that he would lose the territory if it were not colonized, hit upon a plan of granting large tracts of land to such people as would settle it. The boundaries of these tracts were fixed at the coast, but they went inland indefinitely. Settlements were made along the coast.

Some were successful, others not. But the regions away from the coast were ignored. Even today little is known about some parts.

"Well, I could go on for hours about this land. But we've got things to do. Wish I could find some nice secluded spot where we could drop anchor for the night," the missionary said with concern in his voice. "I don't like the idea of stopping within range of arrows, but arrows or not, I guess we don't have much choice while we're cruising this narrow river." He glanced at Tom. "You were asking about the lost stone city, my boy?"

Tom nodded without saying a word and leaned back against the railing.

"Well, according to the document I spoke of, in the year 1600 a Brazilian named Melchior Dias Moreya discovered gold and silver mines. In return for a title—I think it was Marquis, but that doesn't matter—he offered these fabulous mines to the Brazilian government. But for some reason or other he was thrown into prison and his selfish enemies tried to rediscover the mines for themselves. Moreya died a couple of years later, and as far as I know, his secret died with him."

"Boy, it sure would be exciting if the Blue Devil had something to do with all this mystery, Uncle." He lifted his gaze to a pair of bright-colored birds that flapped into the low-hanging branches of some trees that were just overhead and looked at them curiously.

"Isn't a lost oil well enough mystery, Tom?" The missionary's eyes were twinkling. "Well, anyway, in 1743 a native led a group of explorers on a jungle expedition that took eleven years. On one trip, while tracking a white-tailed deer, says the document, the hunters saw a towering chain of mountain peaks."

"What fun! I'm sure glad I'm going to be an explorer, Uncle," Tom said as he leaned forward, listening to every word.

"Well, my boy, I hope you have better luck than most of the explorers who have penetrated these jungle regions." He waved toward the rolling expanse just ahead of them. "But to get back to my story, these mountain peaks seemed to be made of crystal. And in one of them, there was what seemed to be an abandoned mine shaft. On the plateau the party discovered the stone-block city, and on closer inspection, they saw ruins that seemed to be centuries old." He reached out and touched Manolo's elbow. "Take the wheel for a while if you like, my boy." The missionary sat on the railing and seemed lost in thought for a moment.

"That's what gets me, Uncle." Tom shook his head unbelievingly and ran his handkerchief over his moist brow. "This business of buried civilizations

"I'm Going to Be an Explorer, Uncle."

and lost cities. And jumping Jupiter, how could a mountain ever get lost, anyway?"

The missionary went on talking as if he hadn't heard what Tom had said. "Seems that an earthquake had hit the stone-block city and had forced the people who lived in it to leave. But in any case, no bones of any kind were ever found. All that was left were gold and silver, and statues and curious writings. All these things showed that the mysterious people who had lived there all those hundreds of years must have been civilized." The missionary pointed to a cove a few yards ahead and leaned over to whisper something to Manolo. Then he turned to Tom again.

"Well, to make a long story short, the expedition never got back, and never since has anyone been able to see what they said they saw, according to an Indian messenger who—"

Tom brushed back his hair with his hand. "This gets better and better," he said.

"This Indian messenger," the missionary went on, "brought news of the expedition to the Brazilian government. But all in all, those poor explorers are wrapped in as much mystery as Colonel Fawcett, whose story I think you know."

"I sure do, Uncle Leo." Tom rose and began pacing the deck. "I remember all about him. He was the British Army officer who got lost in the jungle—

in this jungle—and whose fate nobody knows for sure. I hope that we—" He glanced around at the gloomy, forbidding wilderness that hemmed them in. "—I hope that we have better luck than Colonel Fawcett and those Brazilian explorers." His frown faded. "On second thought, maybe I'd better study to be a surgeon or a lawyer," he said. "It's a lot safer."

"One of the biggest dangers in this kind of wilderness is getting lost," the missionary said as he trained his binoculars on a low-lying stretch of jungle that led up a hill. "I don't see any hunters' trails around here, and if there aren't any, it means we'll have to hack our way through the jungle with our machetes. And remember, now, Tom. We must be extra careful about staying together." He lowered his glasses for a moment and looked straight into Tom's eyes. His expression was dead serious. "If you get lost in here you are a gone goose. It would be almost impossible to find your way out. The forest looks the same all about you and the thick growth along the waterways is unbroken except by hunters' trails. And even these are quickly grown over if they are not used frequently. Nature covers the marks of man quickly here in this hot moist climate."

Tom nodded without speaking. He sat down on the deck and hunched up his knees. His thoughts drifted back to the fun cook-outs at High Pines, a small wooded section of Duxbury Beach, where he and his friends had often camped out under the stars when they were Boy Scouts. But all this was so different. There were no jaguars or matacaballos or leathery sea turtles at High Pines. There were no hostile Indians like the Blue Devil. His eyes swept the shoreline. They were almost at the cove where his uncle planned to drop anchor. Tom leaned back and closed his eyes. It was all he could do to keep awake.

When he opened his eyes, he saw that Mr. Jason was throwing a fishing line over the side.

"You're not going to angle for fish here, are you, Uncle?" Tom rose and leaned over the fantail as the hook, baited with some of Ozzy's horsemeat, plunked into the dark brown water.

"I want to test this water to see if it contains any food fish," the missionary said. "If it's too acid for food fish it may mean there are no Indians living in this immediate vicinity, because most of them depend on fish for food to a great extent. And if—"

Before he could finish, the line snapped taut and a second or two later a wriggling fish that seemed charged with six hundred volts was lying, squirming fiendishly, on the deck of the *Paloma*.

Tom drew back with a shudder. He saw the murderous rows of razor-sharp teeth in the fish that was about seven inches long. It was one of those dreaded piranhas, which he knew only too well were the deadliest creatures that inhabited either fresh or salt water. At the scent of blood they came up to the surface in large numbers to attack their victim. Once Tom had seen a school of piranhas reduce a huge fish to bones in a matter of seconds.

"Well, that gives us some information," the missionary said. "There are probably Indians not far away. Some Indian tribes are very fond of piranhas. And if there are piranhas here, it means there are other varieties, too, because they need fish to prey on. Of course, I was quite certain there were fish in this secret river, but we might as well be sure." He gestured to Manolo and took the wheel. "I'll nose her in here, boys. There seems to be a trail of some sort leading from this inlet. If there is, we may be on the brink of adventure."

"I guess we won't need the dinghy, Uncle," Tom said. "We can get close enough to jump ashore." He had his eyes glued on what, strangely enough, appeared to be a natural pier, a flat stretch of meadow about thirty feet wide. Suddenly he stiffened. Just above the water line there were rotting timbers. He whistled softly. Here, deep in the heart of the jungle, hundreds of miles from civilization, was a man-made pier, or the remains of what once had been a man-made pier.

"Did you see those mossy-looking piles, Uncle?"

His voice sounded hollow.

The missionary said nothing as the *Paloma* swung alongside the landing. But there was a look of surprise on his face that Tom had never before seen.

CHAPTER FIVE

THE IRON VEST

Mr. Jason jabbed his machete into one of the rotten timbers of the pier. He cut away the crumbling surface layers until he came to the hard inner core.

"Ironwood," he mused. He shook his head slowly from side to side, puzzled by what he saw. "Indians would never build anything like this. White men must have been around here many years ago. This work was done by skilled engineers."

Tom could tell by the grave look on his uncle's face that he was really worried. He turned to watch Manolo, who had jumped onto the jungle wharf. The little Indian poked down into it with his machete. A moment later he looked up, impassive as usual. "Wood under brush," he said.

The missionary was nodding. "It's a regular wharf. I'll say the folks who built it were good engineers. Just look at those timbers." He rubbed his chin thoughtfully. "And you can bet your bottom dollar that they needed special kinds of hard-steel saws to cut through this ironwood." He hit the timber he had cut into with the side of his machete. It sounded as if he had banged against a column of iron or steel. "Well, do you see what I mean? This ironwood is so heavy and durable you'd break an ordinary saw if you tried to cut into it. But as you can see, even ironwood can rot in the steaming jungle. Nothing ever lasts very long down here. No matter how carefully and well man plans, his machinery rusts and the jungle overgrows his roads. This hot, humid climate is one thing that will have to be conquered before the cities we were talking about a while ago can be built."

Tom jumped ashore and examined the top of the pier that Manolo had uncovered. He could see the huge spikes that had been driven through the planking, which originally must have been two or even three inches thick. He turned to the missionary, who was down on his hands and knees inspecting the planking. "Whoever built this pier, Uncle Leo, must have planned to stick around for a while. I thought for a minute we had come to the entrance leading to the lost mountain, but—"

"No, Tom." The missionary put his machete back in its scabbard. "I don't think any Brazilian explorers built this structure. Nor any missionaries, either. But I have a strong suspicion that some highly trained oil engineers, or their carpenters, built it. And it all dovetails with my theory that our friend the Blue Devil has his hideaway somewhere back in there." He made a sweeping gesture toward the jungle expanse around them.

"It sure does all add up, Uncle." Tom glanced at Manolo, who had boarded the *Paloma*. The Indian seemed to show neither concern nor interest in the Blue Devil as he crouched to give Ozzy a dish of evaporated milk. But he knew that Manolo would be the last to underestimate a foe like the Blue Devil. This Indian boy said little. But there also was little that he did not hear and understand. He apparently thought things out for himself and, when the time came to act, he could be depended on to do whatever needed to be done.

"Say, Uncle, those Brazilian explorers who killed off the Blue Devil's family were around here about fifteen years ago, you told us. And doesn't this wooden pier look as if it might have been built around that time?"

Mr. Jason nodded. He mopped his brow as he paced slowly back and forth. "It doesn't take long for this jungle to reclaim anything that is built by man." He kicked into the soft turf overlying the timbers. "This kind of growth would cover up anything in just a few years, but it would take a good fifteen years for ironwood to get that pulpy, I'd say."

"This wood is so hard and so much like iron you'd almost think it would rust instead of rot," Tom said with a smile.

The missionary was absorbed in what he was saying. "But what baffles me, is why any oil engineers would build a wharf in this particular place."

Tom took off his tropical helmet and ran his fingers through his hair. "Maybe so they could haul in their supplies and equipment, Uncle. But it beats me how anyone could haul derricks or big pipes and stuff through this wall of jungle." He peered into a clump of bushes beyond the flat stretch of meadow. "It just doesn't seem likely, that's all."

"They might have brought in their equipment piecemeal and then assembled it later at the site of the oil wells, Tom." The missionary whirled at the sound of something that came crashing through the thicket.

"Only wild boar," Manolo said. "Come nearer I think."

He gingerly leaped back onto the launch and returned a second later with his bow and arrows. It was the only weapon the missionary permitted on the *Paloma,* and it was used only for hunting. Mr. Jason was a man of peace, a medical missionary who depended more on prayer than weapons when confronting the dangers of the jungle.

Tom felt his heart thumping. He watched Manolo glide noiselessly into the underbrush at the head of the pier. The animal sounded as if it were coming directly toward them.

Manolo Brought His Bow and Arrows

"Let's stand by to hop onto the launch, Tom." The missionary's face wore a troubled look. "I'm not particularly concerned about a wild boar, but it sometimes happens that when they crash through the jungle so violently it's because some other animal is chasing them. And the other animal is very likely to be the dangerous one."

Tom scanned the underbrush, shielding his eyes from the sun with the palms of his hands. "Do you think Manolo will be all right in there?" he asked.

"Oh, yes. Manolo is a dead shot with a bow and arrow, and he'll hop into a tree if things get too rough."

Tom kicked a hole in the turf with his sneaker. "I'll never forget the sight of the jaguar chasing that wild boar on our last expedition, Uncle Leo." He walked to the edge of the pier and glanced down at the water. "That started us off on a series of wild adventures, and maybe this boar will be the beginning of our next adventure."

"That was a tapir, Tom, but it's close enough to a wild boar to make little difference." He broke off. "Take a look, Tom!"

Tom saw that the wild boar had broken through the wall of underbrush and was rushing headlong toward them. An arrow was sticking into its side, but it kept coming toward them, grunting and foaming at the mouth. But suddenly it plunged forward and rolled over a moment later when a second arrow pierced its neck. It grunted and honked and squirmed spasmodically, then shuddered and lay still. Manolo was bending over it a moment later. He was a little winded, but he showed no emotion.

"Jaguars," he said softly. "I hear two snarl, but do not see. Gone now." He straightened up and turned to the missionary. "Once trail was there." He pointed into the jungle just ahead of them.

The missionary nodded, as if this confirmed his belief. "I had an idea there might be a trail leading from here. I think we're definitely getting somewhere now, boys." He clapped his hands in his enthusiasm. "If we can read the evidence carefully and be on the look-out for every clue, I think we're going to meet up with our friend, the Blue Devil. We might even discover the lost oil well, although I'm not too much concerned about that." He patted Tom on the back. "But of course if we did find a nice oil well, your fortune might be made."

"I don't want to be an oil baron, Uncle Leo." Tom grinned. "I've decided again that I want to be a jungle explorer. It's a lot more fun." He swept the surroundings with a wondering look. "And no money could ever buy the thrills and excitement you get in places like this."

"You're right, my boy," the missionary said. "This is an exciting life. There is little money in this business, but there are many other compensations."

"I'll certainly never forget these vacations down here, not if I live to be a hundred. Boy, are the fellows back home envious! They all want to be explorers and come down here. If they all do as they want to, we'll know a lot more about this back country in the next few years," Tom told his uncle. There was a twinkle in his eye as he spoke.

"There's plenty of room down here," Mr. Jason said. "And I shouldn't wonder but what there were many fortunes to be made providing the promoters have patience and understanding. For one of the first things anyone must do is to gain the confidence of the native Indians."

The missionary raised his canteen to his lips and drank sparingly. "Shall we have a bite to eat now, or do you first want to take a little stroll through the underbrush?" He rubbed his hand over the stubble on his chin. "This time I don't think I'll waste any time setting up an attraction post. We're after the Blue Devil and his tribe, and I'm dead certain that that scoundrel would turn up his nose at trinkets and colored pieces of cloth. I suspect he's quite a bit different from most of the Amazonian Indians."

Tom grinned. "And besides, Uncle Leo, the Blue Devil seems to have all the blue ribbon he wants." He crooked his elbow and rested it in his other hand.

"I wonder where he gets all his blue ribbon. It seems so silly for him to warn his enemies before he strikes, don't you think?"

"He's that confident, my boy. Some day his over-confidence may be his undoing, too." The missionary was inspecting his knapsack to make sure he had all the equipment he needed. "I really haven't the vaguest idea, Tom, where that jungle gangster got his blue ribbon." He gestured toward the dead wild boar, that was already attracting a swarm of insects. "There's an important bit of evidence. This jungle around here has everything an Indian would want. Fish in the river, wild boar, and probably plenty of other animals that can be eaten. If it weren't for the fact that it would be dangerous to light a fire, we could barbecue the boar tonight. It tastes very much like pork, you know."

Tom glanced up from the diary in which he was making an entry about the death of the wild boar. "Let's see, Uncle, when did Colonel Fawcett disappear?"

The missionary playfully poked Tom in the ribs. "If you try to put that kind of two and two together, my boy, you're going to come out with six. Colonel Fawcett would have a beard six feet long if he were still alive." He frowned, as if trying to remember something. "Let's see, the last jungle expedition Fawcett is known to have organized was in 1925,

when he and his son Jack, and a friend named
Raleigh Rimell tried to get through the jungle in
search of the lost mountain. Wait a minute, I think
I still have the last dispatch he ever sent the North
American Newspaper Alliance at about that time."
He pulled a yellowed newspaper clipping out of his
wallet. "Your mother sent me this clipping many
years ago, Tom. I've carried it around with me
ever since."

Tom's eyes were opened wide. "I wish you'd hurry
up and read it, Uncle. I'm bursting with curiosity."

"Well, here's what Colonel Fawcett himself told
the newspaper that sponsored his jungle expedition:
'Our two guides go back from here. They get more
and more nervous as we push farther into the Indian
country.' "

"Me, too, Uncle Leo." Tom glanced around nervously as if he half expected to find the Blue Devil
watching them with that fiendish look on his face
which Tom had imagined he saw in the sky a few
hours earlier.

"Wait a second, Tom. There's a little more to this
dispatch, if you want to hear it: 'I doubt if it will be
possible to send any further letters.' " The missionary
carefully tucked the clipping back into his wallet, as
if it were something precious. "That was the last
official word received from the party."

"Well, twenty-five or even thirty years isn't such

a long time, Uncle," Tom said as he paced up and down restlessly. "There's a slim chance still that Colonel Fawcett might be alive. He'd be old, but—"

"I admit it's possible, although not very likely, Tom." As he spoke the missionary walked slowly around the pier as if looking for some clue to help solve the problem of how and when it was built. "In 1932 a trapper named Stephan Rattin said he had met a captive white man in an Indian village. He argued up and down that the signet ring the white man showed him tallied in every last detail with the one Mrs. Fawcett said her husband wore when he left her. According to this jungle trapper, this mysterious person said he was a colonel, but he wouldn't reveal his name. One thing he did do was ask Rattin, the trapper, to get in touch with a man in Sao Paulo who had been one of the backers of his expedition."

"Jeekers, what a story!" Tom said. He slapped his thigh. "But what a big scoop it would be for us if we found Colonel Fawcett. I think I'd almost as soon find him as the oil well or the walled city or anything else."

"What about the Blue Devil, Tom?" There was a teasing note in the missionary's voice.

Tom chuckled. "I still say I'd rather find Fawcett. But I guess I'll have to admit that it would be more exciting in most ways to find the Blue Devil."

The missionary was still probing into the turf with

his machete. "I might add that there have been dozens of other reports connected with Fawcett. Parts of his equipment were found, according to some reports, and according to others, he was killed by Indians, as were the other members of his expedition. I suppose that many other explorers have been lost down here, and it is possible that some of them are still alive. But as I said before, the chances of anyone ever finding Colonel Fawcett are very small. We'd better concentrate on the Blue Devil, anyway. He's a handful all by himself."

"You can say that again, Uncle." Tom bent over to see what he was doing. He watched him dig into the black soil with his machete and probe around. A few minutes later the missionary uncovered something that looked like a metal vest. He rose to his feet, excited, and handed Tom the object.

"Do you know what this is, my boy?"

Tom's eyes were bulging out of their sockets. "It looks to me like an iron vest or a coat of mail, Uncle," he said.

The missionary slapped his nephew on the shoulder. "And that's just about what it is, Tom, a bullet-proof vest. And now I really think I know who built this pier. It's common practice for oil engineers and oil company employees in general to wear these vests even today as a defense against Indian arrows. We are not very far from that lost oil well, Tom, which probably means that we are also not very far from the—"

"From the Blue Devil," Tom whispered. Just then darkness descended suddenly on the jungle.

CHAPTER SIX

FISH OR DINOSAUR?

"I'm so excited I hardly feel like eating," Tom said as he set his canvas seat down between his uncle and Manolo. "But this scalloped fish sure tastes delicious." He grinned at Manolo, who was going down into the galley for another helping. "Never saw you so hungry, pal."

"Yes, many moons since I feel like eating," the little Indian said simply. In the darkness Tom couldn't see the expression on his face, but he knew it was placid. Even when the Pomora tribe, one of the cruelest his uncle had ever run into, had kept Manolo guarded by those four fierce-looking harpy eagles, he had never once flinched. The Indian boy rarely looked excited, and he never looked afraid.

"Well, fellow shipmates, I guess Operation Blue Devil begins tomorrow morning." The missionary set his plate down on the deck after emptying the food remnants over the side. He fished his pipe out of his pocket and gave a sigh of relief. He was careful to cup his hand around the match as he lit his pipe, which had a metal cap to prevent the glow of the burning tobacco from being seen. "I hope the jungle hasn't completely wiped out the trail," he said quietly. He turned to Manolo, who was still squatting on the deck eating his supper. "Did you notice any trail markers, Manolo?"

"None." The Indian was silent for a few seconds. "But cut trees show this once was much used trail." He rose and threw his food scraps over the side.

"I'm still wondering about that bulletproof jacket, Uncle Leo." Tom moved his chair closer to his uncle. "It seems odd in a way that anyone would wear—"

"Well, Tom, it really makes sense." The missionary crossed his legs and settled back in his seat. Tom knew this meant he was in a story-telling mood. "Even today in the jungles of Colombia and Venezuela, as well as in parts of Brazil, oil employees and others often wear suits of armor or bulletproof jackets when they leave camp. Especially if they think any Motilon Indians are around." He paused and puffed on his pipe.

"Nobody knows very much about this particular tribe, which has been called the 'world's most unfriendly people.' But we do know that they sometimes roam the jungles in west Venezuela near the border of Colombia. In the twenty-odd years I've been roaming this jungle, I've never come across a trace of a Motilon Indian. All I know about them is that they use no adornments. That would make it difficult for me if I ever did run into them, because I generally make friends with these Indians by giving them trinkets like rings, bracelets, earrings, and so on.

"The men use alligator grease to plaster on their skin to ward off mosquitoes. It is said you can smell the grease along a path where they have recently passed. They are very wise in jungle lore and never become lost. They know that all trees in the jungle bend toward the south and that the branches on that side are heavier and the bark thicker. They have no need for a white man's compass. If they were given one, they would probably use it as a toy."

"Thank heavens there are no Motilons around here," Tom said as he scaled his tropical helmet onto a chair.

"Well, we never can be too sure about this tribe, Tom. All these jungle Indians move around more or less. You never know where you may run into them." He yawned. "Few have ever been captured, as far as I know, and in almost every case I ever heard of, those who were captured invariably committed suicide. They are fierce, proud people preferring death to a life of captivity. I heard of one who killed himself by bashing his head against a wall. Another took his own life by biting into his wrists."

Tom whistled. "What a way to die!"

"And I heard of one case that was even stranger.

One Motilon, who had been tied to a tree by some soldiers during the night, was found dead the next morning. One of the most puzzling deaths I ever heard of outside of murder mystery stories. The doctors who examined his body were never able to determine the cause of his death."

"Maybe he held his breath until his heart stopped beating," Tom said. "Those Motilons are so peculiar I wouldn't put anything past them." He paused. Was that something he heard splashing in the water?

The missionary had already leaped to his feet, and now he was leaning over the railing, trying to make out the cause of the splashing. The moon shone faintly through the lofty trees, casting a silvery light on the coffee-colored river. Fireflies stabbed into the darkness with their yellow polka dots of light. Except for the loud splashing sound, the jungle night hung heavy with silence.

Tom moistened his lips. "My gosh, Uncle," he whispered, "what's going on down there?"

The missionary, still straining to listen, seemed alarmed. He straightened up. "Probably a fish of some kind going after the food we tossed overboard." There was a note of relief in his voice. "Can you make out anything, Manolo?"

"Electric eel," the Indian said.

"My boy, you have the eyes of an eagle." There was admiration undisguised in his voice. "I don't see how you see anything with the moon almost hidden by the branches of those overhanging trees."

Tom looked into the inky water and shuddered. "What a wonderful place for a swim." He leaned over the side to see if he could make out the eel, which could still be heard thrashing around just a few feet away from them. "These piranhas and electric eels sure make swimming a pleasure." He brightened. "Say, Uncle, how does it happen these eels don't have lights, since they generate their own power plants?"

The missionary smiled. "You'd almost think they would, but they're too smart for that, my boy. They like to sneak up on their victims. But I understand that miles down in the ocean there are strange-looking fish that actually do have what seem to be electric lights. And right in this jungle there's a bug that has a red light on one side and a green light on the other. I'm really quite serious. You just name it, and you'll find it in the jungles of Brazil."

"Bugs with green and red running lights." Tom shook his head. "Now I've heard everything, I guess." He yawned again. "But joking aside, Uncle, when are we going to be able to have a nice swim?"

"There will be plenty of time for that later, Tom, so cheer up. But not around here. You can't see them very clearly now, but those trees overhanging this river are what we call assai palms. You may have

"The Jungles Hold Many Mysteries."

noticed the clusters of colored berries hanging from them this afternoon."

"I did, Uncle." Tom sounded bewildered. "But what's that got to do with—"

"Plenty, my boy. Electric eels love the berries, and they have a tricky way of getting to them."

Tom nudged his uncle. "Now listen, Mr. Leo Jason, you are a man of the cloth, and you're supposed to tell the truth at all times. You aren't trying to tell me these eels climb trees, are you?" Tom stretched out flat on his back on the deck and looked up at the crescent moon. "That I just won't believe, Uncle Leo."

"Well, I wouldn't blame you for not believing that, Tom." The missionary sat down beside him. "But quite seriously, the eels give the assai palms such a high-voltage shock the trees quiver like a bamboo shoot in a hurricane. The tree shakes so violently all its berries fall, and the eel, which is a terrific glutton, usually eats them all. While enjoying his banquet he lashes away with his tail, which may be as long as six feet, to keep other fish away. The assai palm is quite common in river shallows, and it makes a perfect set-up for the eels, because its soaked fibres serve as ideal conductors for the eels' voltage."

"Curiouser and curiouser," Tom said, shaking his head from side to side vigorously. "Thank the stars

we don't have any of the critters back home, Uncle."
He pulled himself into a sitting position. "I'll take
salt water any time, anyway. To heck with all these
piranhas and—"

"Even the black panthers that are fairly common
around here are no match for the eels," the missionary continued. "Incidentally, when panthers,
which Brazilians call *oncas,* find hunting poor on
land, they are very apt to prey on fish. I've seen
them sneak down to riverbanks and spear piranhas
in their claws. But now and then an *onca* paws an
electric eel by mistake and bounces back from the
shock. And then it makes a mistake that results in
its death."

Tom sat there fascinated and said, "It doesn't
know enough to run away." His voice sounded sleepy
for he was so exhausted from the heat and excitement
of the day, he had to force himself to keep his eyes
open, even though he was interested in what his
uncle was saying. He noticed that Manolo was
already asleep. The Indian's powers of relaxation
were unmatched.

"That's right, Tom. The panther gets furious.
Then in its rage it seeks revenge. It tries to hook
into the eel's flailing tail with both paws, and this
is just what the eel has been waiting for. He throws
a strangle hold around the panther's neck and pulls
the squirming beast under the water, where he is

completely outclassed. The blood oozing from his wounds attracts the piranhas, which always seem to be on call, and they are only too glad to help the eel devour the carcass if they are not driven away by the flailing tail."

Tom was still struggling to keep his eyes open. "Gosh, Uncle, imagine land and river creatures locked in a death struggle."

"Actually, Tom, the waters teem with life. There is one monstrous fish, the largest fresh-water fish, it is said, that the Indians find very useful. This fish is sometimes almost fifteen feet long and some have been caught that weigh as much as four hundred pounds."

"And that's a lot of fish," Tom put in. "But, Uncle, what do they do with all that fish? They have no refrigeration nor do they have any way of canning the meat."

"They use Nature's way of preserving the fish. Your grandmother used the same method when she wished to keep berries or vegetables for the winter months. In fact this same method is still used. You have probably seen fishermen up on the New England coast dressing their fish and—"

"Do you mean drying the fish, Uncle?" Tom interrupted.

"That's just what I do mean. And you can tell, when you enter an Indian camp if they have had a good catch—by the smell. And these Indians make use of every bit of their catch. They use the dried tongue for a file and the large scales make a fine sandpaper used in polishing their weapons."

"Gosh!" exclaimed Tom. "I'd hate to get a piranha or an electric eel on my fishhook. I think I'd just drop the pole and run."

"Yes, my boy, and even the last members of the dragon family—the heavy-mailed alligators—fear electric eels. We may see some of them before long in broad daylight. They look something like yellow serpents as they skate along the river's surface. When fording with animals, the natives down here have to use harpoons to keep them off. They—"

He broke off as something ponderous crashed into the portside of the launch. For an instant the *Paloma* shivered as if it had been rammed by a whale. Tom, just a moment ago on the verge of falling asleep, leaped to his feet in wild excitement. Manolo, awakened by the terrific jolt, had also jumped up as the *Paloma* shivered for a second time. What in the world was happening?

"Steady as you go, boys." The missionary gripped Tom and Manolo by the elbows. "As dangerous as it is, we'd better use the flashlight to see what's going on," he continued quietly. "Let's take it easy, boys, and be ready to leap ashore in case the launch capsizes. This water is no place to be with electric eels flailing around."

For a third time the *Paloma* shook from the impact of something crashing into it. Tom nodded as the missionary signaled for him to follow him and Manolo ashore. Miscalculating the distance in the dim light, he landed in the water a few feet short of the pier. Panic seized him as he came to the surface. He heard something churning in the water just a few yards away. He reached for the slippery pier and tried to pull himself up, but again he slipped back into the dirty water that was so full of deadly enemies. He slipped under the surface for a second time as his uncle's voice trailed off.

"Here, Tom, here!" the missionary shouted. "Take hold of my hand. Reach straight up." Tom reached in the direction of the missionary's voice and grabbed his hand. In his wild imagining he thought he felt something slimy brushing against him— against the back of his legs. He felt himself being hauled up, now limp from terror and exhaustion.

"That . . . was a close . . . squeak," he murmured. "Too . . . close for comfort."

"Take a quick look, Tom." The missionary turned the beam of light on a huge black object that had its monstrous-looking head raised above the water, as if it were studying them. Tom could make out nothing very clearly until his eyes became accustomed to the brightness of the light. And then he saw something he had never seen or heard of before. It was an animal with a huge head and with fierce-looking eyes that seemed too small for that calflike head.

"Jumping Jupiter," he whispered. "What is that terrible-looking zombie, Uncle? It looks worse than those sea serpents you're supposed to see in nightmares."

The missionary nodded in agreement. He glanced around him. He was worried at the prospect of some unfriendly Indians spotting the light. "I hope the cover of trees is thick enough to hide this light," he said. He ran the beam of light over the humped back of the fish. "This fellow is one of the biggest fish-oxen I've ever seen, Tom. I have heard that they are sometimes found as long as seventeen feet, and this one is close to that."

"What a nasty-looking specimen," Tom whispered. "No wonder those oil engineers picked out this spot for a landing pier, if the water is deep enough to contain a whopper like that." Tom glanced into the muddy stream and shuddered at the close call he had just had. He had no idea how dangerous fish-oxen were, and he didn't want to know, either. If he knew the truth, he might not be able to sleep tonight.

He watched the monster disappear under the surface, leaving an ever-widening circle of ripples.

"I guess it's okay for us to go back on board now, boys," the missionary said. "And you don't know how lucky we are that that fish-ox didn't capsize the *Paloma*. If it had, it would certainly have been curtains for us."

CHAPTER SEVEN

A WARNING

Early the next morning, Tom, his uncle, and Manolo prepared to explore the jungle near the pier. They took food—sardines, crackers, chocolate bars—things that were nourishing but light and easy to carry. They planned to return to the *Paloma* for the evening meal and so did not carry much with them.

"Here is some pepper," Mr. Jason said, handing each of the boys a box of ground pepper.

"Thank you, Uncle," Tom replied, puzzled, "but I don't like pepper on anything I'm taking with me."

"Take it anyway, my boy," Mr. Jason said, smiling at Tom's amazement. "It may come in handy. If we should meet up with some unfriendly natives and we get in a pinch, a well-aimed handful of pepper will start them sneezing and give us time to get away."

"Well, if that's the case, I'll take it," Tom said, still smiling. "But that's the queerest weapon I've ever heard of."

They filled their canteens with fresh water and

left the launch.

The old hunters' paths were overgrown, they found, and vines and brush had to be cleared away. Tom led, and for a while his machete swung rhythmically back and forth. The growth along the water was dense and heavy, but they saw that it cleared somewhat as they got to higher ground.

Tom's arms hung heavy at his sides and his breath was coming in short gasps now. The dazzling morning sun had changed the matted jungle into a steam bath, and the heat now was almost more than he could bear. He rested his machete on the ground and turned to look for Manolo and the missionary, who were bringing up the rear. This was no fun, he thought as he mopped his dripping brow. It was real work hacking your way through this kind of jungle.

"Take it easy for a while, Tom, and let me handle the machete," the missionary said. "I have a hunch that our going may be a little easier once we get away from this swampy section." He started slashing at the underbrush as he spoke.

Tom grinned wearily at Manolo, who was carrying his knapsack as well as his own. "This is one time when I wish I were a squirrel or a monkey," he said. He waved at the overhanging branches. "It's a lot easier traveling up there, don't you think?"

Manolo seemed too preoccupied to listen. He had

They Hacked Their Way Into the Jungle

his eyes fixed on the stump of a tree, and Tom
could tell that something was brewing. He watched
his Indian friend chop a near-by tree with his hand
hatchet and study the rings. Tom was fascinated. He
knew what the clever little Indian was up to. He
was counting the rings that reveal the age of a tree.
Then by comparing the age of the tree with that
of the stump of a similar tree, he could get a rough
idea of the number of years that had elapsed since
the tree had been cut. Very clever. Tom stood there,
his hands on his hips, waiting for him to finish
counting.

"Stump is six years old." Manolo tapped the fresh
stump of the tree he had just cut with his hatchet.
"This one nineteen years old. If two trees planted
same time, that one near you is cut thirteen years
ago."

The missionary turned and nodded approvingly.
"Nice work, Manolo. And it's just about what I
figured. I remember now that it was about thirteen
years ago that a British oil company tried to lay a
pipeline somewhere around here. From any information I could gather, the workers had such a tough
time with dengue and malaria and other tropical
diseases, they made little progress. The jungle was
too powerful a foe for them, and as matters turned
out, many of them who didn't die from tropical
fevers were murdered by prowling Indians."

"Sometimes I wonder if this place will ever be civilized," Tom said. He glanced around at the forbidding wall of underbrush. "And if it is, humanity can thank people like you, Uncle Leo, who spend all their lives trying to make things better for other people."

"Thanks, my boy. I really don't do very much." He paused for a moment to listen. "But as I was saying, these Britishers had tough sledding. There was a saying that about twenty white men were killed for every mile of pipeline that was laid." He stooped and pushed his way through the passage he had just made. "Say, here's wild pineapple and a clump of coconut palms. More and more I'm beginning to think the Blue Devil belongs to the Motilon tribe."

Tom looked puzzled and interested at the same time. "Why?"

"Well, for one thing, the Motilons love wild pineapple, boar, deer, tapir, monkey meat, and alligator eggs, and so far we've seen all of these things around here except deer, tapirs, and alligators. Probably all of these can be found somewhere not far away. We haven't as yet explored much of the country. Food, of course, is one of the things very necessary to life, and you will find that people the world over live near the source of their food supply. That was true of many of the tribes of American Indians. One of their reasons for moving about was their search for adequate food. When food became scarce in one section of the country they moved on to a place where it was more plentiful."

"We haven't seen any monkeys around here yet, have we, Uncle Leo?" Tom said.

The missionary smiled and pointed. "Take a look up there, Tom." He indicated a towering coconut palm. "Can you see who's watching us?"

"Leaping greensticks, Uncle, two of those preacher monkeys!" He was entranced by the sight of these peculiar jungle inhabitants. "I haven't seen one of them since we hunted the Pomora tribe last summer."

"Just see them scampering around up there, Tom. Look how they stare at us and jabber. Do you suppose they are trying to give us a message of some kind?"

"I'll bet they are, Uncle." Tom grinned as he hacked away with his machete. "They are probably warning us to keep out of their domain. I'll bet they hate intruding white men just as much as the Blue Devil is supposed to. See those black buzzards up there? They've already caught the scent of the boar's carcass."

"Right you are, Tom."

Tom shaded his eyes and studied the large birds that were always ready to swoop down on dead or dying creatures of the jungle. Odd, he reflected, these vultures thrived on other animals' misfortune. Filthy buzzards they were, that preyed on rotten flesh, on carrion. Yet, he supposed, they had their place in nature's plan. They did help to keep the jungle clean. He shuddered at the thought that came into his mind. If anything happened to him he wondered if these same buzzards would swoop down and start pecking at him with their curved beaks. What a ghastly thought!

He remembered the hundreds of buzzards he had seen hovering over a slaughterhouse on the outskirts of Belem, the fascinating city that was less than seventy miles south of the equator in Brazil. And he had seen them on the roofs of houses right in the residential sections of Belem, roosting like chickens on a coop back home. Motilon Indians and buzzards were sure unpleasant things to think of. One killed you, and the other saved the undertaker any trouble.

"Say, Uncle, just who are these Motilons, anyway?" Tom slumped wearily against a tree and mopped his brow. "If you think there's a chance that we are invading their domain, or that the Blue Devil belongs to their tribe, I'd better know something about them."

"I've really told you just about all I know about them, Tom." The missionary sat down near Tom and leaned against a tree. He was panting after his exertion. "Guess I'm not as young as I used to be.

Say, what's this?" He reached to one side to pick up something.

Tom walked over curiously. It looked to him like any ordinary piece of steel. But then he noticed it was pointed.

"It looks like a tool or weapon," he said excitedly. "But where could these people get steel? Where did they learn to use it? And what did they use it for? An arrowhead?" In these jungles steel weapons seemed as unlikely as automobiles in the Stone Age. The smallest touch of civilization in this tremendous wilderness was a thing to cause wonder and amazement. Tom examined with awe the small roughly shaped piece of steel.

"The plot is really beginning to thicken, Tom." The missionary was still nodding in answer to Tom's question as he held out the arrowhead so Tom could see it. "I had heard that the Motilons had gone modern to the extent of tipping their weapons with stolen iron and steel fragments, and here we have what looks like proof. It's a piece of metal, really, that was used to tip one of their arrows, which are generally made out of ironwood or black palm. You remember that I told you they used huge bows that are from six to eight feet long."

"How could I ever forget?" Tom took a sip from his canteen.

"Many of these Indians, and probably the Motilons as well, make several kinds of arrowheads. There are small, blunt-pointed heads for shooting birds, larger sharp ones for hunting the larger animals—tapir, deer, jaguar, and others—and then the war arrows that are often treated with poison. Often they cover these poison arrows with a guard until they are ready to use them. Really, Tom, these Indians must be very busy, for all these arrows must be made by hand with the very simplest kind of tools."

"I suppose they are busy, but they are far from friendly, aren't they, Uncle Leo? Their ideas of fair play are different from ours."

"They hide behind trees and bushes and usually shoot their arrows from close range. And they can pierce a man's chest with their arrows. From all I've heard, they appear to wait until a worker has passed, then hit him in the back. Well, boys, we'd better keep hacking."

"How long have these Motilons been living in the Brazilian jungle, Uncle Leo?" He rose and began hacking again. They had to cut a path if they were going to get any place.

"According to the experts, they've been thriving in these jungles for about four hundred years, my boy." He pulled out his machete. "Incidentally, there are a couple of rather interesting legends about them. According to one legend, they were originally

Germans who—"

Tom turned and held his machete poised. "Are you serious?"

The missionary nodded as he hacked into a prickly growth. "The story goes that in the first part of the sixteenth century, Charles V of Spain, who was then Emperor of the Holy Roman Empire, ordered—"

"Wow, Uncle, how you know your history!" Tom whistled his amazement. "I don't see how you remember—"

"Well, I'm not too sure of all the details, but it seems that King Charles handed some Motilon territory over to some Germans, for a reason I forget at the moment. The Germans sent some soldiers into the jungle to collect the debt. Some of these adventurers deserted to hunt for El Dorado, which—"

Tom ran the back of his arm over his brow and paused briefly. "That's the fabled golden city, I take it."

"Right. Nothing was ever heard of these deserters, by the way. Then the legend goes on to say that the German soldiers ran into some Carib women and married them. Their descendants became the Motilon tribe."

"That's quite a story, Uncle." Tom turned and grinned at Manolo. "I'll sure be glad when you get your strength back, Manolo. You're much better with a machete than I am."

"Not true," the Indian said. "You much better."

"Why don't you take it easy for a while, Tom," the missionary said. "There's another legend that the Motilons are the remnants of the fierce Carib Indians who were never conquered by the Conquistadors. But anyway, few persons have any trustworthy idea about them. We don't know whether there are fifteen hundred of them or fifteen thousand. One American explorer who came down here with his wife to try to track down the Motilons stayed for more than a year. And what do you think?"

"He never saw any," Tom said.

"Bull's-eye. Not a one did he see. But he did learn something about them. From the size of their footprints he guessed they are of average height. I remember this scientist saying that they were the only people he knew of anywhere who had no dogs."

Tom pushed his tropical helmet back on his head. "Funny, I never thought of that." He studied the curved blade of his machete. "Even Eskimos have dogs."

Mr. Jason nodded his head wearily. "I wish we knew as much about these Motilons as we do about Eskimos. But we do know that their malokas, or jungle houses, are usually about fifteen miles apart, and that each one forms a separate community. Often the whole family—father, mother, children, grandfather, grandmother, perhaps uncles and aunts —live in one large hut. Each family has its own place to hang its hammocks, and each cooks over the common fire in the center of the crude building."

"I suppose when there is nobody else to fight they squabble among themselves." Tom gazed dreamily up into the blue tropical sky. His thoughts were far from Duxbury, now. What a wonderful storyteller his Uncle was, he reflected. When he came back to his senses he noticed that his Uncle was smiling at him. "Say, Uncle Leo, didn't you say those malokas are shaped something like Quonset huts?"

"Roughly the same, Tom. And it's in these malokas that the tribal chieftains live." He sneezed. "I think my hay fever is returning. Some scientists have said that except for the tribes in the deep interior of New Guinea, the Motilons are the most primitive persons in the world." He put his machete back in its scabbard. "I think we better stop now and have some chow. We'll keep working until just before twilight sets in. Then we'll go back to the boat. We don't want to be caught in Motilon territory around dusk, because these Indians are most likely to attack during the dim twilight hours of sunrise or sunset. Remember that they have kept oil companies out of their domain, so we can't be too cocky about our prospects of getting close to them."

Tom looked startled. "Close to them, Uncle!" His

hand froze on the canteen he was about to lift to his lips. "You don't mean we—"

The missionary handed him a bar of chocolate and a can of sardines he had just opened. "Not exactly that, Tom. But I do hope we'll get close to the Blue Devil, because he is the key to the whole Motilon mystery. That is, if he is a Motilon, as he seems to be." He yawned and stretched. "Once we make friends with him we'll be doing society a service."

"How come?" Tom munched thoughtfully some crackers he had taken from his own knapsack. "You mean that fewer white persons will be murdered?"

"Yes." The missionary was silent for a moment as he ate a sardine. "But I mean more than just that. I want to bring Christianity to these savages. I'm not so concerned over the fact that they control land rich in oil, gold, copper, castor beans, copra, vanilla, Brazil nuts, and black palm. That is none of my business. Maybe white men have no right to them, I don't know. But I am worried over their desire to live as outlaws without the grace of God." He stopped abruptly, a look of alarm on his face. "Say, where did Manolo go? I've been waiting for him to come and have a snack with us. Have you seen him in the last few minutes?"

Tom caught the note of worry in his uncle's voice, and a sudden fear gripped him as he rose to his feet. He remembered Manolo's last disappearance. Yes, and he remembered the long agony of the search through the jungle, and how at last they had found the little Indian sick and wasted away in the Pomora camp, where the eagles that were guarding him had been straining at their bonds in a desperate effort to devour him. Tear him to pieces and devour him . . .

"Shall I call, Uncle?" Tom's lips were trembling as he waited for Mr. Jason to tell him what he should do.

"Wait a moment, Tom. This takes some thought. It might be too dangerous to call." He glanced around cautiously. "Just a minute or two ago he was standing near that tree." He gestured toward a palm tree. "It isn't like Manolo to romp off by himself in the jungle without telling us where he's going." The missionary sucked in his breath and paced back and forth restlessly. "No," he said slowly, "it isn't like him." He whirled at the sound of something fluttering. "What was that noise?"

"Just a few parrots up in a tree there, Uncle." The beauty of the gleaming yellow and green birds was lost on Tom. He could think, and with growing dread, only of his faithful little friend who had come to be like a brother to him. He felt so helpless. What could they do? If they could only shout. As his eyes swept around he thought of the words of his uncle: "You never know, when you are in the jungle, what murderous eyes are watching you from behind the nearest tree, and what kind of monster will crash out of the thicket."

Suddenly his eyes bulged. He drew in his breath and tried to speak, but no words came. On the branch of a tree about ten yards ahead of them something was fluttering in the gentle breeze. It was a piece of blue ribbon!

CHAPTER EIGHT

THE ABANDONED CABIN

Tom brushed away an insect that almost entered his open mouth. The whole business was incredible. In fear and trembling he watched the piece of bright blue ribbon fluttering there so innocently on a branch. It was tied in a nice neat bow. The Blue Devil was hurling his defiance! It was a warning that he was ready to strike at any moment.

Tom saw the stunned look on his uncle's tanned features. Everything that the missionary had said about the Blue Devil came back to his mind now. A diabolically cunning Indian, who glided like an invisible phantom through the shadowy jungle—a fiend who mocked his victims before he killed them. He turned numbly when his uncle tugged at his arm.

"Let's get back to the launch as quickly as we can, Tom." There was an unaccustomed hoarseness in the missionary's voice. "I have a feeling that some Motilon eyes are watching us right now. Those devils can rush through a jungle without snapping a twig."

"But poor—Manolo, Uncle Leo." Tom dabbed at the hot tears that were streaming unashamed down his cheeks. "After all he's been through, and—he's—he's still so sick and tired and weak—" He could say no more. He struggled to keep from sobbing. He wasn't so much worried about what was going to happen to him, now, but poor Manolo!

The missionary put his arm around him as they hurried along. "We're in a bad trap here, Tom." He glanced over his shoulder as he spoke. "If we want to do all we can to help Manolo, our best bet is to try to make the Blue Devil think we've gone, then sneak back after dark. Come on."

Tom trailed along with a feeling of numb hopelessness and despair. But he knew in his heart that his uncle was right. If they tried to press forward through the wall of thicket that loomed ahead, they would lose any chance they had of rescuing Manolo. And it wouldn't be the first time they had rescued him. It was the little Indian's courage and daring that got him into all this trouble.

But how could Manolo have disappeared so completely and so suddenly? He had been with them only a few minutes before. Someone going through the forest as silently as only an Indian can go, must have carried him off.

"But where could he have gone?" Tom asked again. He still felt that it was almost impossible for anyone to disappear so completely and so quietly.

Tom hurried unseeing down the path they had

come. The very air they breathed seemed heavy and oppressive. What did the bushes beside the path hide? What fate stood waiting for them?

Tom paid no attention to the briers that scratched his face and arms as he ran, now, after his uncle. Suddenly the missionary stopped and pulled Tom around a bush that on closer inspection looked as if it had welcoming arms stretched out.

"There's one of those killer plants, Tom." There was horror in the missionary's voice. "It's kind of gruesome to see, but just take a quick glance at the ground near the bush."

Tom felt a sinking sensation in his stomach. There, at the foot of the killer plant, was a pile of bones, including what looked like a human skull. Tom gasped, too overcome to say anything.

"Probably one of the oil engineers who was trying to make an escape," Mr. Jason said. "That skull looks too large to have belonged to a monkey."

They rushed from the scene and kept running. Their only thought was to get back to the pier and the *Paloma* as fast as they could. There they could rest a little while and prepare to search for Manolo after dark. When they came to the turf-covered pier by the river they stopped short. They could scarcely believe their eyes. It was a few seconds before the full weight of his uncle's words struck him.

"Tom, Tom, my boy, we are hopelessly trapped."

"That's a Man-Eating Plant!"

He gestured sadly toward the placid river. "The *Paloma* is gone." The missionary stood at the river's edge like a frozen statue. "It doesn't make sense, Tom," he said in a hoarse whisper, glancing furtively around as he spoke. "It was moored fast just a couple of yards from here." He stamped with his foot. "And now—now—it's—gone—"

Tom raised his canteen to his lips and took a convulsive sip. He knew he had little water left, and he had no idea where he would find more drinking water now that the *Paloma* was gone, but his lips felt parched. The intense tropical heat was taking its heavy toll of his strength. The odds against them were lengthening. Here was the end of the long trail of jungle adventure, in a bleak region that would still preserve its mystery after they were murdered. Tom looked up at the sky mechanically. His mind was haunted with thoughts of those filthy buzzards which would be quick to come on the scene when disaster struck.

In the distance he saw the black approaching cloud that would unload its downpour any second now. He had been so confused a moment ago when he thought of his emptying canteen that he had forgotten all about rain water. He could collect some, as he had often done before, in his tropical helmet. But water was only one of hundreds of worries. He felt a surge of anger at their helpless and hopeless situation. It just wasn't fair, somehow. He and his uncle were pitted against phantoms, shadows—silent shadows that moved through the jungle the way the shadow of a near-by tree was moving past them now. It was a pitiless enemy they couldn't fight, because they couldn't see him—or them. There might be hundreds, or there might be thousands of these silent enemies. Tom started at the shadow a huge butterfly cast. Any minute now he expected to hear the mocking laugh of the Blue Devil. He was sure this jungle gangster had a mocking laugh and lips that curled into a sneer as he surveyed his helpless victims through narrowed eyelids.

"It was those black buzzards, I'd bet, that gave the Blue Devil the tip-off, Tom," the missionary whispered as he gripped his nephew's arm. "He must have been somewhere in the vicinity, and when he noticed the big birds circling over a certain spot he knew that something or somebody was dead or dying." He pointed at the bloodstains and bones on the ground, the evidence the vultures had left after their feast on the remains of the wild boar that Manolo had slain. "As far as these Motilons are concerned, every trifle is a clue. Every twig, every leaf, a broken-down clump of grass, little things that anyone else wouldn't even notice, give a message to these people who depend on the forest for their very existence."

Tom bit his lip. He felt so unhappy and frustrated.

He watched a slow-moving ripple back slowly against the pier, soon to be followed by several more. He glanced up at the assai palm, saw the berries raining down as the tree shook. There was not enough wind to shake the assai palm like that. The electric eels were after another meal. If they were attacked from the rear, it would be dangerous to try to swim across this tawny river, which was teeming with deadly fish. Soon the river's surface would be placid again, hiding all evidence of the fantastic creatures that lay beneath.

Tom kicked savagely at the turf. They might never know what happened to the *Paloma* or to Manolo. And Ozzy, where was his pet baby ocelot? He swallowed. He knew his eyes were glistening like the dew on the morning branches. Everything he loved and needed was being snatched away by the cruel hand of an unseen enemy.

"Uncle Leo—" He averted his gaze. "Since there's only one thing we can do now, we might as well do it. We have only enough food to last us for a few days, and there's only one direction we can travel now." He jerked his thumb up the trail. "It's safer to go that way than to try to swim across this stream, with all its piranhas and electric eels and fish-oxen, and stuff." He suddenly thought of something. "Say, Uncle Leo, you don't suppose that fish-ox drove a hole into the hull of the *Paloma* and made it sink, do you? He looked big enough to do it."

The missionary, now reassuringly calm and deliberate, shook his head slowly. "No, my boy. If that had happened, there would be things floating around here in the water. I don't see a sign of any flotsam. In the first—" He broke off abruptly as a movement caught his eye. Ozzy had just come out of a clump of bushes and was rubbing against Tom's legs. "This," he said hollowly, "is too much. Look, Tom!"

"I—I—I see, Uncle, I see." Tom's numb gaze rested for a moment on the blue ribbon neatly tied around Ozzy's neck. He stooped down, picked up a stone and slammed it into the river. Why didn't this Blue Devil kill them outright, instead of taunting and torturing them? Was this his idea of a game?

The missionary was kneeling, stroking the fur of the ocelot as if it were a tabby cat. "Looks as if you've had enough to eat, Ozzy," he said affectionately. "Now if you could only tell Tom and me who fed you, and what you had to eat—"

Tom's eyes were glued on the ocelot. Did he notice something his uncle was paying no attention to? He was sure he did. Ozzy was trying to get their attention, trying to tell them something. There was no doubt about it! Ozzy was trying to persuade them to follow him. He would stalk away a few feet, turn, then return. He kept repeating this process patiently.

"Uncle—Leo, look at—Ozzy. He's trying—"

The missionary rose as if he were in a trance. Then the frozen expression on his face melted into a broad smile. "Of course, Tom. Manolo—Ozzy is trying to tell us where we can find Manolo. Manolo, like you, was always so good to him, and—"

Without waiting to see whether Tom was following, the missionary trailed the jungle kitten down the path. Tom felt jubilant. He had a feeling that in Ozzy, a wild creature of the jungle, he and his uncle had finally found an ally—the ally they had so much needed. He wanted to burst into song. For one brief instant he forgot completely the threat that the Blue Devil offered. Even that fiend would never take into account the instinct of a jungle kitten like Ozzy. A fiend like the Blue Devil, who would never dream of treating a wild creature with kindness, would never know the loyalty that was so often given in return.

They paused while Ozzy sniffed at the bloodstains on the path before he continued stalking toward the path they had hacked. Neither Tom nor his uncle breathed a word.

The rain was beating down heavily now, and the sudden afternoon darkness gave Tom a new feeling of hope and security. He felt cool and refreshed and protected. Here, at last, was the supreme thrill of his lifetime. He had all the confidence of a blind man following his seeing-eye dog. He paused behind his uncle a few yards before they reached the edge of the trail they had cleared. Ozzy was sniffing again. Then he swung to the left of a clump of briers and disappeared beneath them. Tom, his heart pounding and his breath coming in short gasps, stooped to follow the missionary who was parting the heavy branches.

"You're sure that's not another of those killer plants, Uncle," he whispered. He shuddered at the thought of getting trapped in the tentacles of a shrub that acted like a murderer.

"Shhh . . . I'm positive it's not." The missionary had turned and now he was touching his lips with his fingers to warn him to be as quiet as possible.

He pushed his way through the thicket. For a moment, with the rain dripping down, beating its familiar tattoo, he found himself in a sort of dark tunnel. He slogged along in a silence that was broken only by the patter of the rain. A moment later he found himself in a clearing. Here was a fairly well-defined hunters' trail. He could see Ozzy a few yards ahead, proudly leading the silent procession. Here was a jungle creature, he thought, that had been tamed by love and devotion. And all those strokes of kindness, all the milk and meat they had given him, were now being repaid in full. It almost seemed as if Ozzy was taking care of them instead of being cared for!

The trail was leading over a rise now, twisting its narrow way between walls of foliage that Tom was unable to identify. For what seemed another seven or eight minutes Tom followed along. He felt slightly weary, although he was spurred on by the excitement he sensed lay ahead.

"Sorry," he whispered. He bit his lip. There he was talking again. He backed away after bumping into the missionary. He had been so absorbed in thinking about the Blue Devil he had forgotten to watch where he was going.

"Shhhhh, Tom. Not a word," the missionary whispered. He gestured toward Ozzy. "I think we're getting somewhere."

Tom went over the series of events that had led up to this dramatic moment. The disappearance of Manolo, the sight of the blue ribbon on the bough, and the disappearance of the *Paloma* seemed to have made no sense until now, and it was Ozzy who was making it make sense now. The whole mystery, he told himself, would soon be solved one way or another. There was only one thing he could be sure of. The Blue Devil was certain to be lurking around somewhere not too far away. But was Ozzy leading them to Manolo or to him?

Tom halted when Mr. Jason suddenly stopped. A short distance ahead of them, nestling among the overhanging branches of lofty trees, he could see a run-down thatched hut. It looked crumbly with age and uninhabited. But just inside the door he made out a hammock, and in it was a sleeping form.

It was Manolo!

CHAPTER NINE

A DARING PLAN

Tom wanted to scream and leap up and down with joy, but he nodded at his uncle's signal to keep silent. He knelt down beside the missionary, and together, they surveyed the situation. Except for Manolo, who was apparently sound asleep, there was no sign of life on the place.

Tom rubbed his chin thoughtfully. Why was the Indian boy sleeping here so peacefully? He wasn't tied up or anything. Had he lost his way and decided to rest until he regained his strength, or what? No. None of these things was likely. There was something strange about the whole business. Manolo would never leave them like this unless he had a good reason.

"Drugged," the missionary whispered half to himself.

"Of course," Tom told himself. Of course his pal was drugged. He would not otherwise be sleeping there in a strange hammock so casually. Tom glanced at the faded brown hammock that looked as though it was ready to fall apart any moment. It was probably another relic that was left by one of the oil engineers.

"Now what, Uncle?" He watched Ozzy push his way through the screen door, leap onto the hammock, and lick Manolo's face. Then the affectionate ocelot dropped to the floor and crouched there.

"Yes, I'm sure Manolo is drugged, Tom. The Blue Devil somehow captured him and left him here while he ran off with our launch. And thanks to Ozzy, I think he has played right into our hands. Never underestimate the cunning of a jungle cat."

"I get it, Uncle." Tom's confidence was returning fast, but he reminded himself that the odds shifted back and forth constantly in this jungle game of trying to outwit a tricky enemy. "We can just wait around here until the Blue Devil returns, then grab him."

"That's the general idea, my boy." He took his nephew's arm. "Let's take a closer look at Manolo. But be careful, very careful. Remember that we are no match for the Motilons on their home grounds. Never forget for one moment that they know every hill and valley, every twist and turn of this their own territory. From childhood they have been taught to walk stealthily through the forest. They have learned early to move quietly and to hide themselves from any prying eyes. We shall have to be especially careful if we do not want to end up as captives of these wary natives."

"You never know, when you are in the jungle, what murderous eyes are watching you from behind the nearest tree, and what kind of monster will crash out of the thicket." Tom found these words his uncle had once spoken again returned to his thoughts like a warning refrain.

He went with his uncle into the small hut. He could tell by the way Manolo's lids were pressed down against his cheeks that he was sleeping an unnatural sleep. Instinctively, he reached out and felt the little Indian's chest. He could feel his heart beating, thank heavens. Manolo was very much alive. His chest heaved rhythmically. Tom reached down and stroked Ozzy while he glanced around, as if half expecting to find the Blue Devil grinning at them.

"I'll take another look outside," his uncle said, going out of the hut. Tom nodded. A moment later he ran to the door, startled by a sudden sound. His uncle was nowhere to be seen! Tom glanced wildly around at the rain-soaked underbrush and trees. Everything looked so ghostly and bleak—and so suddenly threatening. His first impulse was to call for his uncle, but he checked it. He had another sinking feeling. He was sure, now, that they had fallen into some kind of trap. It wasn't Ozzy's fault, of course. But unwittingly, the jungle cat had led them into what was beginning to look more and more like a deadly trap.

"Manolo's Been Drugged!"

First Manolo was missing. Then the *Paloma,* their only means of escape. And now—now—his uncle was gone! Tom's eyes fell dejectedly on the sleeping Manolo. Two fifteen-year-old boys—alone in an unknown wilderness haunted by a cunning Indian. And one of them sound asleep.

What should he do? Where should he go? For a minute he stood still and looked about him. There was no sign of anyone or anything. Where had his uncle gone? How had he disappeared so quietly? Had some native taken him captive or was it the Blue Devil himself who had carried the missionary away?

Tom crawled on his hands and knees to the edge of the clearing. He felt he would be the next victim. He ran his eyes around the dark, rain-soaked underbrush, looking for that frightening piece of blue ribbon. No sign of it. Not—yet— Dusk had fallen without his realizing it. Here he was in the dark and in the rain, without a ray of hope. That's how it was when you tangled with these treacherous Indians. Up one minute, down the next. He looked around with fear and trembling. It was so quiet he could hear the faint ticking of his wrist watch. He crawled into the nearest clump of bushes and lay face down, his face resting on his elbows. He felt a drowsiness stealing over him and he tried desperately to shake it off. Sleep might be fatal, now. There was a slight chance that he might be able to avoid being captured by the unseen enemy long enough to do something about rescuing his uncle and Manolo. No, this was no time to quit. He simply had to do something. He shook his head sadly. But what? What?

He started crawling back toward the thatched cabin. This must be where the oil engineers had lived, he thought. It was a long narrow shelter. Now in the rainy darkness he could make out no further details. All he could hear was the rain beating a steady tattoo on the trees and the shelter. He rose slowly and tiptoed toward the shelter. The screen door was open as he had left it. Manolo slept peacefully in the hammock, but, to Tom's despair, Ozzy was gone. He entered cautiously. There was a musty smell suggestive of decay. He took out his flashlight, knelt down, and ran a beam of light on the floor. In one corner was a pile of rusted tin cans. He moved the beam of light across the rotting wooden floor. He was suddenly aware of a whirring of wings of some kind. He switched off the light, but then curiosity overcame him. He felt frantic as he focused a beam of light on several bats that were now flying out of the screen door. They were going foraging for their evening meal of insects. What did the presence of bats in this abandoned cabin mean? That it was uninhabited by humans? Not necessarily. Bats were fairly common in houses even in South American cities.

But what kind of bats were they? Were they the harmless, really useful kind, that fed on insects? Or could they be the vicious little creatures that attacked men in their sleep? Tom's uncle had told him of these bats that attached themselves to a sleeping person. They knew just where and how to find the veins without the person being aware of their presence. Then they quietly drained the life blood from their victim. Stories have been told of people waking in the morning almost too weak to rise. Could it be possible that this Blue Devil kept such vicious creatures to torture his enemies? Such a thing could be, for had the Pomoras not used the alligator bug to torture their captives?

Suddenly Tom stiffened. Although he had heard no sound other than the whirring of the bats' wings, he was sure there was someone besides Manolo in the room with him. He could feel the cold sweat stand out on his forehead. In the darkness he could see nothing. Should he snap on the light again and find out once and for all whether his imagination was playing tricks on him again, or what?

He drew back against the damp wall, terrified. As he stood there trembling, he heard a slight rasping sound that gave him even worse shivers. The rusted screen door was opening! Talk about ghosts—

Tom let out a shriek and snapped on the light. He saw nothing but the door closing with that ghostly sound. Maybe it was just the wind, he tried to tell himself. His imagination was running riot again. He even thought he could hear a mocking laugh. It was a war of nerves. The Blue Devil or some other phantom of the jungle was playing with him the way a cat toys with a mouse before devouring it.

Tom clutched at his throat, found his breath coming in gasps again. He was more overcome with fatigue than he had been before, but he dared not lie down to rest. Never before had he felt so completely alone, or in such an utterly hopeless and dangerous situation. A frantic urge to open the door, rush out, and retrace his footsteps seized him, but he realized he could not abandon his loyal friend, Manolo. And then, too, where could he go? His jumpy nerves left him with a feeling of jitteriness he just couldn't shake off.

"Steady, Tom Stetson, take it easy. You've been in scrapes like this before, and you always got out of them. Getting—panicky—won't do you any good." He wearily rubbed the back of his hand over his eyes. He was so jittery he was beginning to talk to himself. "Wait a minute, Tom." Tom found himself laughing nervously at the way he kept talking to himself. But his confidence again came surging back as one of the most daring plans he had ever conceived entered his head.

The boldness of the idea left him quaking, but

why not? If it went off successfully, it might be the only possible way of rescuing his loved ones. A hoarse squawking sound just outside the door sent him crouching back against the wall again. What kind of creature made that eerie noise? He cocked his ears. Again that raucous, harsh noise that sounded like a death rattle. It was surely an animal of some kind. It must be. But the suspense—the suspense was almost more than he could bear. He crawled along the soaked floor and pushed open the door. The sound was coming from a near-by tree. He crouched under it for a few seconds and tried to make up his mind what to do. Again that ear-splitting cry.

Tom aimed the beam of light at a place in the tree from which the sound seemed to come. There was a loud fluttering of wings, and out of the tree came what to Tom looked like a mammoth black and yellow oriole. But it was almost as big as a crow. Nobody ever saw an oriole that big! Tom felt his heart pounding as the bird hovered in the path of light, squawking even louder now, as if it were angry because its peace had been disturbed. It was a cacique, Tom suddenly remembered. There was another sound of fluttering and a second bird appeared and flew straight up out of the ray of light provided by the flashlight. Then it suddenly descended and seemed to be heading straight for him. Tom shrieked and raised his arms to shield his face from the giant bird's talons, but it swerved just as he could almost feel its wings brushing against his arms. It was probably as terrified as he was!

Tom backed away. He tried to remember something about the cacique's habits. All he knew was what his uncle had told him—that they were twice as noisy as crows and that they built their nests in trees. Their nests were big—about eighteen inches in diameter. They were made out of woven grasses, and hung from the branch tips.

Tom reached down for a stone and was about to heave it at the birds when he recalled one curious habit these caciques had. Sometimes they boldly constructed their nests near human settlements, but never without taking unusual and uncanny precautions. They used a nest of angry hornets as a nucleus for their colony when they built their nests in an inhabited territory. What could be cleverer? An idea struck Tom.

It was another wild idea, but if it worked it would give him a clue as to whether this region was inhabited or not. If the hornets were up there it meant there were humans in the vicinity!

Tom drew back and let a stone fly. It glanced off one of the caciques, which let out an ear-piercing shriek and flew off into the night, followed by its squawking mate. Tom stooped to pick up another stone, and trained the light with his left hand while he heaved the stone with all his strength. Again no sign of any hornets. He repeated the operation a dozen times. He was finally ready to quit when he heard the angry buzz of a swarm of hornets, whizzing furiously in the path of light. Tom felt jubilant as he turned and rushed into the shelter. But his joy was short-lived. If the area was inhabited, how did he know whether or not he was surrounded by enemies at this very moment? And there might be just one inhabitant or two or thousands.

But now the daring plan he had conceived a few moments ago was shaped. It was a desperate last hope, but it had to be tried. He would substitute himself for Manolo in the hammock, pretend he was drugged, and thereby put the Blue Devil off guard. It was the only way he could think of if he wanted to get to the bottom of the mystery. The chances of getting away with the hoax were slim, but what other chance of salvation was there, with his uncle gone, Manolo out of action, and the *Paloma* either stolen or lost? He might as well go down fighting. Unless he found his uncle, and unless they found the launch, they were doomed anyway.

He bent over Manolo. He could tell from his deep breathing that he was still unconscious, still drugged. He picked him up carefully and took him behind a clump of bushes where he propped his head on his

Tom Threw a Beam of Light at the Tree

tropical helmet. He covered him with some mosquito netting. He could see from the welts on his face that he had already been badly bitten. The ground was soaked, but that made no difference now. Manolo was already sopping wet. Besides, there was nothing else he could do.

Tom returned to the thatched hut. He stopped and listened intently. He was alert to every movement—every leaf that moved with the breeze that had sprung up with the sunset, every twig that crackled. There was no sound but the soft dripping of the drenched foliage and the gentle sighing as the breeze stirred the trees. Apparently no one had seen him move Manolo. Tom breathed a sigh of relief. He was safe for the moment—until the unseen enemy made a new move in this deadly game of hide-and-seek.

Tom sank down on the hammock and closed his eyes. There was nothing to do now but wait. He didn't know exactly what to expect, and he felt so utterly drowsy that he almost didn't care. It was impossible to keep his eyes open. His last thought before he fell sound asleep was whether the Blue Devil or one of his tribe would find him in the hammock and mistake him in the darkness for Manolo. The only chance of success was to have the Indian or Indians return during the night. It had to be done before morning, and Tom promised himself that he would wake up before morning came.

He settled comfortably in the hammock just before he dropped off to sleep. There was no need at the moment to pretend to be drugged. He was sleepy enough to seem drugged.

CHAPTER TEN

INTRUDER IN THE NIGHT

Tom awoke, startled by the sound of a shriek of agony. He lay there for a while stupefied, too numb with horror to move. Where was he and what was making that terrifying racket out there?

He grabbed the sides of the hammock and jerked himself into a sitting position. It was dark and wet. Suddenly he realized where he was and what he was doing. He was in the mysterious, abandoned shelter that was inhabited by bats—and maybe by Indians, he couldn't tell for sure.

He dared not move from the hammock. He cocked his ears as the shrieking just outside the shelter continued. It was no animal this time, but the frenzied screech of a human being. His throat felt parched and he felt weak from the lack of food. He took a short sip of water from his canteen. Who was that out in the bushes, and what was he yammering about?

The answer to his question burst on him. The swarm of hornets had apparently found a victim, and they were giving him the business. And who could this victim be but an Indian? It certainly wasn't Manolo or Uncle Leo. It might be—it might well be the Blue Devil.

Tom lay back in the hammock, clutching at his throat. Tensely, he listened to the wailing sound of someone suffering horribly. He had always thought of Indians as rugged men who had nothing but contempt for pain. The person out there sounded like a coward. But then he remembered the words of Uncle Leo: "When an Indian whoops and hollers he may be hurt, but it isn't too likely as far as some tribes I know are concerned. It's more likely that he's awfully mad at something." Tom closed his eyes. He could feel his heart thumping heavily as the door opened. He held his breath for an instant.

He was sure the sound of his heart pounding against his chest could be heard. He heard the door swing shut, but no further noise. But now he was conscious of the fact that somebody was bending over him. He felt the hot breath of a panting human.

He did his best to imitate the breathing of Manolo, to give the intruder the impression he was still under the influence of a drug, as Manolo was.

"Good. Still asleep," a voice said.

Tom started. He had expected to hear the voice of the Blue Devil, or some other Motilon, speaking in Indian dialect. He had no idea who this person could be. His thoughts ran wild. Colonel Fawcett? No, absurd. Here was the voice of a much younger man. It must be one of the oil engineers who somehow escaped the clutches of the Motilons. But that wasn't very likely, either. Tom wished he could open his eyes and take a quick look. But that would be too much of a risk.

He continued his unnatural breathing as the seconds that seemed hours passed. Odd, what an effort it was just to lie down and try to breathe. You'd think it was so easy, but— What was that? Was he mistaking his own breathing for—no. There was someone else besides himself in the room who was breathing. More than just that there was a loud snore. Tom, himself, kept breathing as before. No use taking any chances. He would have to be sure the intruder was sound asleep before he took any further steps.

Tom listened intently. There it came again—a deep, prolonged snore. Tom's ears almost ached from straining to hear any small sound that might give a clue to what was going on about the cabin. There was no other noise except the rasping chirp of some night insect and the swish of a branch across the thatch as the breeze swept through the clearing.

Tom cautiously changed his position in the hammock. The rope that hung over the hook squeaked —loudly, Tom thought. Had the sleeper heard the noise? Tom held his breath for a moment. There was the snore again. The rhythm had not been changed. It had not disturbed his sleep.

As he lay there, tortured by curiosity and weak from hunger, he wondered what had happened to his uncle. He imagined him lying somewhere on the wet ground, murdered. And once more came the dreaded thoughts of those buzzards, omens of evil. He tried to shake off the grim thought. The time for action was near, he felt. He could hear the loud snoring of the intruder a few short yards from him. Cautiously, Tom opened his eyes. He slowly raised his head and turned to look in the direction of the intruder. The rain had ceased now, and there was enough moonlight in the room to enable him to make out a shadowy bulk that looked like a hammock. He hadn't noticed it before, and perhaps it was just as well. He might have made the mistake of using it to cover Manolo. And if that hammock were missing, the Indian would have known that something was wrong.

Tom surveyed the room, keyed up to the drama of the situation. Here was his golden opportunity. The intruder was dead to the world, no doubt of that. The hornets had probably sapped his strength. The first faint light of dawn was streaking into the abandoned cabin now, which meant that it would be light in a minute or two. Tom thought fast. There was no more time for dillydallying.

His heart skipped a beat when he shot a hurried glance toward the door. Leaning against the wall beside it was a long black bow, and beside it was a bundle of black arrows. Black palm! Tom was sure of it. That was the kind of wood the Motilons used for their bows and arrows! And as he expected, the bow seemed to be about eight feet long. What a murderous-looking weapon!

Tom probed for the floor with one foot as he kept his eyes on the hammock. He could now clearly see the form that was sound asleep in it, but from his position he could make out few details. He couldn't tell whether it was a white man or an Indian. The stranger was slumped too deeply in the hammock for that.

Tom was ready to spring toward the weapons, if necessary, but he decided it would be better, if possible, to tiptoe quietly and grab them. He knew that he couldn't use them as they were meant to be used, for these huge bows could be used only by someone who had had a great deal of practice and had become skillful. If he took the bow and arrows he would deprive the sleeper of his weapons and, perhaps, Tom could find some other way to use them. What a swell club that sturdy-looking bow would make!

He stepped onto the floor and backed toward the weapons. He felt in a better position, now, standing between the stranger and the door where the weapons were. He was almost certain that the man in the hammock was a Motilon, but seeing was believing!

He put an arrow against the bow in case the stranger awoke too soon, and then he sneaked toward the hammock. He paused every few steps to make sure the man was still asleep. A quick glance upward showed him dozens of bats curled up in sleep on the rafters of the shelter.

There he was! The man in the hammock was the best-looking Indian Tom had ever seen. He was a copper-colored, perfectly proportioned athlete, not too tall, but tall enough. It was hard to tell his height, the way he was sprawled out in the hammock. Tom studied his powerful-looking legs and arms, with their bulging biceps. The Indian had long, black, straight hair, and a strong well-shaped nose that might have belonged to a movie actor. He was an Indian, all right, but he looked as if he might have had some white man's blood running through his veins. His features were those of a white man dyed copper.

The thought of the story his uncle had told him about the German soldiers of adventure who had so mysteriously vanished in the jungle flashed through his mind. But now was not the time to dwell on such thoughts. He fingered the huge bow and studied the Indian's placid face. He was sure that the man in the hammock was the Blue Devil!

Tom felt cruel as he raised the ponderous bow to strike. He had never done anything like this before, but did he have any choice? He held the bow poised in mid-air. Weren't the lives of his uncle and Manolo at stake, as well as his own? But even as he hesitated, the thought came to him that this, after all, was not the best course of action for him to follow. What good would it do to knock this Indian senseless and tie him up? He was a Motilon, which meant he would be stubborn. He would very likely refuse to talk, and that meant that Tom might never discover the whereabouts of his uncle. No, there must be a better way. He would put Manolo back in the hammock the way he was originally and let the Indian think that nothing had happened.

His best plan of attack was to let this Indian lead him to his tribe, which was probably not too far away if those caciques, which had built their nest close to a hive of hornets, could be trusted. After all, he had to find Uncle Leo. And he also had to find out what had happened to the *Paloma* if he ever hoped to escape from this backwater country. He was on the ragged edge of nowhere, and he knew it.

He put the bow and arrow back where he had found them, after putting Manolo, still deep in sleep, in the hammock. The Indian must have given him a huge dose of drug. Tom stole cautiously past the tree where he could see no trace of the hornets, now. He followed the twisting trail that led past an enormous tree. Tom shaded his eyes and glanced up

Tom Held the Bow, Ready to Strike

into its branches. It surely was an odd-looking tree. There were no branches for about a hundred feet up. It had a tremendous trunk that looked as if it was more than ten feet in diameter. Tom continued a few yards down the trail and sank down on the ground against another tree. Here he could see what was going on in the cabin without being seen himself.

As Tom relaxed, he found he was hungry. It was no wonder for he had had little since early yesterday morning. He opened his knapsack and looked in. There was not much there—a tin of meat, some more crackers, and a box of pepper that his uncle insisted he carry as a sort of weapon.

He took the top off the tin can of meat he had been hoarding for an emergency like this and leaned back lazily against the tree. It was the first time he had really relaxed for the past two days. But he was certain that something was going to happen soon. His eyes dreamily followed the large red and green parrot with a long tail that had just fluttered out of the branches at his approach. Wait a second— it was not a parrot. It was a macaw. He could tell by the naked space around its eyes and by its long tail. Its presence reassured him, for it meant there were Brazil nuts near by. And he might have to depend on nuts and tropical fruit to keep from starving. He had little food left in his knapsack. The macaw disappeared from view, giving its harsh call as it went. What an unmusical bird! Tom leaned back and closed his eyes.

A moment later he was fast asleep.

CHAPTER ELEVEN

TREETOP OBSERVATORY

The noon sun was streaming through the towering treetops when Tom awoke with a start. He opened his eyes and stretched as he sat there, yawning. For a moment he wondered why he wasn't asleep in his bunk on the *Paloma*. Then the events of the day and night before came back to him. The Indian intruder who spoke such perfect English—Manolo, lying drugged in the hammock. Tom rolled over and rested his head on his elbow while he peered through the foliage at the abandoned cabin. He had been asleep for almost four hours. What if the Indian had left!

Tom jumped up, terrified at the thought of losing the trail of the key figure in a mystery that became more and more baffling.

He stole cautiously toward the shelter. For a moment he paused at the breath-taking sight of colored birds flying overhead in a V-shaped formation. They were too high up for him to make them out clearly, but he guessed they were some species of parrot. There were millions, maybe billions of these birds in Brazil. They were of every color of the rainbow, and many different sizes. What a place this Brazil was, Tom thought as he watched the birds. It was a paradise for wild animals—and wild Indians.

He pushed up the trail with one eye cocked on the arresting sight in the bright blue sky. How, he wondered, did so many birds know enough to fly in such perfect formation? But now what was happening? The birds had suddenly broken formation, and were now scattering in all directions. Tom felt his jaw sagging. What did it mean?

He knew a moment later. So that was it! Out of the sun, now directly overhead, he saw a huge harpy eagle gliding on outstretched wings. It was much bigger than any of the four eagles he had seen guarding Manolo in the camp of the Pomora Indians. It was driving the birds right down into the lofty trees just a few yards ahead of him. Tom trained his binoculars on the eagle and watched the fascinating hunt. He saw the eagle clearly now. It seemed to be checking its swift descent as it plummeted into a flock of the squawking birds. They were macaws, Tom could see. Red, green, yellow, orange, purple, and many other colors. What a sight! It looked like an explosion in a paint factory. He wished he had his camera so he could take some colored pictures. They were close enough for that now.

Tom shot a glance at the cabin, now just ahead of him. The squawking was loud enough to wake anyone sleeping normally. If the Indian wasn't awake yet, this was sure to do the trick.

Tom gasped as he looked up again. The eagle, now directly overhead, appeared to be about five feet tall. It had one macaw in its curved beak, two more in its powerful-looking talons. Tom watched it soar in a spiraling flight, circle, then suddenly dive into the top of the huge tree he had noticed earlier that day—the tree with no lower branches. So that's where the eagle had its nest!

Tom wished he could get a close look at the nest. He remembered his science teacher in high school telling him that an eagle's nest might weigh as much as a ton, although the bald, or golden, eagle's nest weighed only ten or twelve pounds, he had said. And the harpy eagle's nest was around fourteen pounds. Eagles return to the same tree year after year and, instead of tearing down the old nest as many birds do and building a new nest, the eagle simply adds to his old nest. In this way, over a period of years, a huge pile of sticks and grasses is accumulated. On closer inspection, the eagle he had just seen dive into the towering tree near by was no ordinary harpy eagle. It was too big for that. It looked like one of the giants of the species, that built nests that measured about three feet across and a foot deep. They consisted mostly of loosely woven sticks. Tom tiptoed toward the screen door of the cabin. He had a healthy respect for eagles, after what his science teacher had told him. It was sometimes said that eagles carried rabbits, sheep, and even larger animals to their mountain nests, but all that talk of their carrying off human beings was the bunk, Mr. Janes had said. But Tom could now vouch for the fact that he had seen an eagle carry off three macaws.

There was not a sound in the cabin. Nobody was snoring. And Manolo was no longer in the hammock on the other side of the screen door! What a fool he had been to sleep so long! The Blue Devil was gone, and he had taken Manolo with him. He peered through the screen door. He was gone, all right. And so were his black palm bow and arrows.

Tom went in and looked around. He felt blue, but after all, he couldn't help it. He was human, and he had gone for a long time without sleep. He simply was unable to wake up in time. His glance rested on a rusted heap in the corner. He stooped to pick up a rusted object. A coat of armor! There were five or six of them, piled there. This thatched cabin must have been built by the oil engineers, all right. This was all the evidence Tom needed, now. There was no possible doubt about it. He was in the domain of the Blue Devil.

Tom was on his way toward the door when he saw something on the floor that brought him to a halt. It was a tiny piece of blue ribbon. "The Blue Devil, all right," he whispered. He picked the ribbon up and examined it. It was tied around a button. Tom studied the button on his own shirt. It was the same kind exactly. And Manolo wore a similar shirt. His Indian pal was giving him a clue. Then he must have awakened and realized his predicament. This was no warning from the Blue Devil. It was a message of hope from Manolo.

Tom studied the piece of blue ribbon again. It looked as if it had been torn hurriedly. Somehow the little Indian had got hold of the ribbon, and he was tearing off small pieces. He was using them as trail markers. Tom no longer felt that he was pitted alone against the powerful forces of the forest. He had an ally, now, in Manolo. And right now Manolo was probably in the Blue Devil's hideaway. Tom leaped high in the air and slapped his hands against his knees. Here was the first bit of good news he had had for a long time. And if he knew Manolo, there would be similar clues strewn along the hunters' trail that surely must lead to the hideaway of this fiend—the Blue Devil.

Tom rushed outside and headed down the trail. He kept his eyes on the ground, looking for other pieces of blue ribbon. A few yards down the trail he found the first piece. He pursed his lips in a silent whistle as he walked along. The full force of the sun was beating down, and, as usual, it made a steaming

Turkish bath out of the soaked jungle. But here a heavy overhang of branches and liana vines shielded him from the bright glare. It made a world of dancing shadows and half-lights—that's what the Brazilian jungle was.

Tom halted abruptly. He felt like whooping with joy. There, right smack in the middle of the path, was a third piece of blue ribbon. Tom picked it up and glanced behind him, as if to make sure that nobody was following or watching him. Things were looking up, for a change.

He felt confident that when he reached the Blue Devil's hideaway he would find his uncle and Manolo. And they would be alive, he felt sure. If the Blue Devil wanted to kill them, he would have already done so. He had had plenty of opportunity. Tom ran his hands through his hair. He really had no idea whether his uncle was dead or alive, but he suspected the Blue Devil was holding him, like Manolo, until he found out what they were up to. Tom's thoughts drifted back to Ozzy. If he found his pet, too, he would ask for little more. Except to find the *Paloma,* of course.

The fourth piece of blue ribbon was on the trail leading to the enormous tree where the eagle had its nest. Tom, bewildered by this sudden development, glanced up at the tree. He inched along slowly, now, alert to the least sound that would tell of someone near by. He thought of the summer before, when he had stumbled on the lookout station of the Pomora Indian chief. It had been built high in the loftiest tree in the area. Had the Blue Devil selected a similar lookout tower in that tree just ahead? And if so, what was the connection between the Blue Devil and the eagle?

Tom moved forward cautiously toward the tree. There were no more bits of ribbon. Perhaps Manolo had used all the pieces he had had. He mopped the perspiration from his brow. A few minutes later he came to the clump of foliage that separated the trail from the huge tree where the eagle had its aerie, or nest. Tom took off his helmet and rubbed his forehead with the back of his arm. He glanced idly at the spider monkey, a tiny little thing no larger than a kitten, that hopped from limb to limb on a near-by tree. He studied the wall of underbrush.

He had a feeling that he was close to the secret hideaway. All the evidence he had had so far led to this spot. And the presence of the eagle meant something he was sure. He snapped his fingers. The eagle acted as a sort of glorified watchdog! Maybe that was it!

Tom backed up and shielded his eyes with the palms of his hands as he studied the tree. Who knew what mysteries those spreading branches hid? His imagination took him to the backlands of British

Guiana where, said Uncle Leo, there lived a mysterious tribe who made their homes in camouflaged
treetop dwellings. And in those lofty homes they
spent most of their lives. It was not even necessary
to come down in order to travel. They moved about
by swinging along the vines that hung from tree to
tree throughout the jungle. The men even carried
their weapons and the women carried their children
while traveling from place to place. Tom was sure
that this tree was the key to the mystery.

He cautiously approached the thick, matted underbrush that hid the bottom of the tree from view.
He parted the bushes and pushed forward in the
dim light. There was no clearly defined trail that he
could see. A moment later he found himself in a
clearing at the foot of the giant tree. And right there
on the ground, plainly to be seen, was another piece
of blue ribbon!

Tom's heart was beating wildly. He felt that finally he was at the end of a long search. But every
big mystery, it seemed, had a lot of little mysteries.
How, for example, did anyone get into this tremendous tree? Its lowest branch was at least a hundred
feet above the ground. He was sure of that now. It
was a perfect spot for an eagle's nest, but for humans—

Tom stepped back into the brush at the side of
the path directly beside the big tree. Why he did it

he was not sure, for he had heard no noise nor had he seen a sign of anyone. But he sensed danger and felt safer when hidden in the brush.

Tom shrank back into the underbrush just in time. He could hardly believe his eyes, but there it was! Part of the lower tree swung open as if it were a revolving door. Out of it stepped the same Indian he had seen sleeping in the hammock in the thatched hut. He had his first really good look at an Indian he could now be sure was the famous—or should he say infamous—Blue Devil.

The Indian glided through the underbrush and vanished. He made no sound as he went. It was uncanny that so large a person should make no noise. Tom's eyes were bulging as he looked at the doorway that was cut into the tree. He waited for a few minutes, fearing that the Indian might return. Then, treading as softly as he could, he hurried toward the tree and pushed the secret panel open. He found himself in a narrow, dark corridor barely wide enough to permit passage. It led to the other side of the tree. It must have taken weeks, he thought, to carve such a passageway through this tree. It was high enough so that he could walk through without stooping. He flashed on his light. He half expected to find a secret stairway, but he was disappointed. He walked out the opposite side, after pushing open another panel that worked like the first, and looked for

The Blue Devil Suddenly Appeared

the next clue.

There it was—a thick liana, or vine, cable that hung down from the branches above. Without taking time to look around, Tom, in his excitement, seized the liana cable and started pulling himself up. He was used to this kind of climbing, and it was lucky he was. He would have to hurry, for there was no telling when the Blue Devil would return to his hide-out.

Up and up he went, hand over hand. "One-a, two-a," he grunted. In a pinch he could cut the Blue Devil's access to this tree, he thought, merely by cutting the cable at the top. And then how would he get down himself? Time enough to think of that later, he told himself. Beads of perspiration covered his forehead. But he was encouraged as he glanced up. There, above him, he saw what looked like a crude log cabin. There was the end of the mystery at last. But it was not necessarily the end of his trouble.

He peeked into the room, not knowing what he would find. He hoped to find Uncle Leo and Manolo, but there was always the chance he might instead find some Motilons. But the room was completely empty. His heart sank. Where were his friends? He hopped onto the floor. In one corner was a roll of blue ribbon. Beside it was a collection of bows and arrows. He swept the room with a troubled look. The floor was made of intertwining liana

branches, much thinner than the liana cable. So were
the walls and the ceiling. He looked out one of the
many openings. What a perfect view! The Blue
Devil apparently did not live here all the time. It
was his lookout station.

Tom marveled at how completely the lookout
cabin had been hidden. No one would have dreamed
that up among the protecting branches a building
as large as this could be constructed. Tom examined
the floor and the walls. The weaving of the floor
must have taken a great deal of patience for the
vines were all of one size and were perfectly matched.
Although the Blue Devil had neither nails nor car-
penter tools, he had constructed a solid, substantial
building with only those few materials that the
jungle offered. This unusual Indian must be a busy
man from all appearances, for it must have taken a
lot of time to build this structure.

Tom leaned out and looked at the liana cable dan-
gling beside the tree. If the Blue Devil should return, as he might at any minute, what would happen? Odd, in a way, that the Indian was unarmed
when he left his tower. It was a good sign, though.
It meant he was off his guard, that he didn't think
he was going to run into any trouble. It was reassur-
ing, at least, to know that he for the moment held
the high cards. Again he nervously glanced down at
the liana cable to make sure the Blue Devil wasn't

coming up. Then he rushed from one opening to another to see if he could figure out what the treetop retreat was used for, besides an observatory. And finally he found the answer.

CHAPTER TWELVE

THE HIDE-OUT

There was another stout liana cable leading through the branches to another tree. One much smaller than this one, but one that was still much larger than most of the trees in the area. Without a moment's hesitation he stooped down and grabbed the cable. He began to swing himself hand over hand toward the tree. He was panting when he pulled himself onto a branch. Just above it was a larger cabin, similar to the one he had just left. He peered into it. As soon as his eyes became accustomed to the shadowy light he saw the most welcome sight in years. Uncle Leo and Manolo!

"Tom! It's you! Thank God!" Tom was too overcome to say a word.

"Yes, Uncle Leo, here I am at last." He saw at a glance that Uncle Leo, like Manolo, was tied up. His arms were tied behind him, and he was lying on his back in what seemed to be an uncomfortable position. And the smiling Manolo was trussed up the same way.

"You will never know how glad I am to see you, my boy." There were tears in the missionary's eyes as Tom untied his bonds. "The Blue Devil kept asking Manolo and me where you were, but we pretended not to know anything. The only reason he has not yet killed us, he said, was to make us help him find you." He glanced at Manolo. "He would have a long wait, I fear."

Tom struggled to keep his glistening eyes from showing. "Mr. Jason, I presume," he said. "And it's so nice to see you, young man. Did you say your name was Manolo?" He pulled the little Indian into a more comfortable position and at the same time brushed away a tear of happiness.

The missionary had rolled up into a sitting position, and now he was rubbing his arms and legs. He looked anxiously at Manolo. "Take it easy, my boy. Don't try to move around until your circulation returns." He smiled broadly. "In one way, Tom, nothing could be better. Here we are, all three of us, in the private den of the Blue Devil. I think he's in for a little surprise. But how in the world did you—"

"Don't give me credit for anything, Uncle Leo." Tom's eyes rested on Manolo admiringly. "Give our pal, Manolo, here, all the orchids. If he hadn't dropped all those pieces of blue ribbon along the trail, I probably would by this time be the main course for those buzzards." He sank down beside the missionary. "And I'll bet Manolo didn't say a word about his clever trick."

The missionary shot an affectionate glance at the Indian, who seemed embarrassed. "Not a word," he said. He turned to Tom. "What is all this about Manolo showing you the way?"

Tom told his uncle of his leaving Manolo in the hammock, of his own nap in the forest, of his return to the cabin only to find it empty. Then he told of the mail vests he had found and of the button with the blue ribbon.

"I was pretty sure that although the Blue Devil seems to have many white man's tools he would not have a button exactly like the ones on Manolo's shirt and mine. That is what made me think that Manolo was sending a message and why I looked for more signs. But what has been happening to you all this time?"

Uncle Leo turned to him with a smile.

"I thought you would be asking that before very long," he said. Then he paused.

"Tell me, Uncle," Tom said anxiously. "I really would like to know."

"Well, the last thing I remember before I came to my senses here was that you and I followed Ozzy to— By the way, Tom, where is Ozzy?"

Tom averted his gaze. "I'm sorry, Uncle. He just disappeared." He felt choked up again.

"You don't think—you don't think that Ozzy will go back to the jungle, do you, Uncle?"

The missionary struggled to his feet and rested his hand on Tom's shoulder. "No, Tom, I don't think that. But I wish I knew where he was."

"I just don't know what has become of him. He wasn't in the hammock when I took Manolo out last night and he hasn't appeared this morning. Do you suppose the Blue Devil has taken him to some other hide-out? What could have happened to him, Uncle?" Tom sighed. He felt a bit guilty that he had not thought of his pet this morning.

"I wouldn't worry about him, Tom," his uncle said. "He has probably been out in search of a meal. He has been with us long enough, though, to remember that his meals are given to him on the *Paloma*. He'll find us again, never fear."

Tom looked straight into the missionary's eyes. "If anything happens to Ozzy, Uncle, I'll never get over it." He paced back and forth. "By the way, Uncle, how did you get up here? You don't mean to tell me the Blue Devil carried you while he hauled himself up that cable?" His eyes were popping.

"I don't know for sure, my boy. But after seeing his powerful physique I wouldn't be the least bit surprised. I do know he carried Manolo up." He shrugged. "And he must have done the same with me. He could probably be an Olympic shot-putter or discus thrower if he felt like it. He's a superman if I ever saw one." A troubled look came into the missionary's eyes as he rubbed his chin thoughtfully. He walked to one of the openings and glanced out. "I guess I must have been drugged after I was knocked out. I remember something hitting me, and nothing more until I woke up here. But what a headache I had. And Manolo complained of the same thing." He smiled. "He didn't complain. But he admitted his head hurt a little when I questioned him." He looked down at Manolo, who was sitting with his knees hunched up, his eyes on the floor. "What's the last thing you remember, Manolo?"

"Waking in hut." He smiled wanly. "Someone put me in hammock, and when I open my eyes I see Tom going away from hammock and out of door." He brushed his hand across his brow. "Then I hear snore, so I know someone else is there. Maybe Blue Devil. I keep very quiet because he might wake. I feel too weak to walk by myself and do not want Tom to carry me, so I stay there and pretend I still sleep. Then I leave blue ribbon for Tom to find."

"It's just like you to think of the other fellow, Manolo." Tom made no effort to hide his affection. "But tell me, where did you find the blue ribbon?"

"On *Paloma*." The Indian smiled. "The only blue ribbon I can find is one used for tying package. I take it because I think it may come to help when we meet with Blue Devil."

"Very clever, Manolo!" the missionary said, patting him on the shoulder. "There's nothing like giving the enemy a little of his own medicine." There was a catch in his voice as his glance shifted from Manolo to Tom. "I want you to know that I'm mighty proud of you both." He paused at a rustling sound, felt relieved when he realized it was only the afternoon wind brushing through the branches. "And now, boys, we have our work cut out for us." He looked at Tom. "You say he walked past you down below?"

"Right, Uncle. He was probably out on the prowl for me."

"Well, our best bet is to suppose he will return any moment." The missionary leaned against the wall and pulled a handkerchief out of his pocket. "We are three against one, but that's not the point entirely. Knowing these Motilons as well as I think I do, I'd say it would do us little good to overpower him and make him surrender, assuming that we could do that. The *Paloma* has disappeared, and it's my hunch that only the Blue Devil knows where it's gone. The chances are that he'll never tell us if we try to use force on him."

Tom paced back and forth nervously. "I guess you're right, Uncle Leo. I just didn't think of this angle." He looked out the opening. "And he may

"I'm Proud of You, Manolo."

return any second. I don't like the idea of having him get to his bow and arrow before we get out of here."

"What do you mean, Tom?" The missionary looked alarmed.

Tom gestured toward the other cabin. "They're over there."

"Oh," the missionary said thoughtfully. "Then that probably means that he is not far away. I doubt if he would be gone very far or very long from his weapons."

"What do you think we had better do, Uncle?" Tom asked. "Should I go over and bring them back here? Or should I take them and hide them in the brush somewhere?"

The missionary was lost in thought for a moment. "Well, for the present anyway, we'd best leave them alone. If he found them missing he'd leave and be back in no time with members of his tribe. I hate to have to say it, but we have only one course of action." He rested his hands on Tom's shoulders. "And it's going to be dangerous for you, my boy. For us to leave now would be suicide. We are lost without the *Paloma,* as we've said so many times before. The Blue Devil must have it hidden somewhere. When he comes back he must find us just as we were when you found us. Lying down here, tied. He has already told me that no harm would come to us until he found you. How he knew you were with us is not hard to imagine. He must have been watching us from behind the bushes when Ozzy led us to Manolo. But he was alone at the time, and he figured he could handle only one of us at once." He ran his hand through his thick white hair. "I'll wager he's out looking for you now."

"Tell me what to do, Uncle. We haven't too much time." Tom kept looking toward the other cabin as he spoke. He felt that at any moment the Blue Devil might appear. He looked about this lookout trying to find some other means of escape. But there seemed to be no other exit but the liana vine that led to the other lookout in the eagle's tree.

The missionary's face was troubled. "It breaks my heart to have to say this, Tom, but I think you should leave us right away. Go down the vine cable, which I imagine is the only way of getting up here. And that's a good thing to remember." The missionary leaned out of one of the openings. "It's a long drop from here. Like dropping from a six- or seven-story building."

Tom tightened his belt. "I think I must have lost a few pounds in the last two days, Uncle Leo." He looked at Manolo, who was lying on his side resting his head on his elbow. "I guess all of us could use a good square meal."

The missionary nodded sadly. "I know, Tom. I

know. And all our good square meals are on the *Paloma*. But it's odd—neither Manolo nor I feel very hungry. Must be the drug. The Blue Devil is clever, but if we're extra careful, I think we'll outwit him." He put his arms around his nephew. "You'd better go now, my boy. Hide somewhere near the foot of the tree, and when the Blue Devil goes off on a hike again, you'll have to trail him." He tightened his embrace. "And for heaven's sake, Tom, take no chances. We're in a jam, but we'll get out of it without taking unnecessary chances." He waved toward the little Indian. "Manolo and I will lie low and play dumb. And when you get a chance come back up here and tell us what you've found out!" He rubbed his cheek thoughtfully. "Somehow, Tom, you've got to find out where the Blue Devil has hidden the *Paloma*."

"Okay, Uncle, I'll be off for now." He reached down and patted Manolo on the back. "Take it easy, old pal. I'll see you soon."

He left without another word or backward glance. He didn't want them to see how troubled he felt, or let them see the tears in his eyes. He knew he might never see them again. And leaving them like this, completely at the mercy of a jungle assassin, went against the grain. But he had no choice in the matter. He was about to lower himself onto the liana bridge when he remembered something. He watched them adjusting their vine bonds, to make them look as if they had been undisturbed. "Uncle Leo, one thing. Have you noticed an eagle around this tree-top? I—"

"We certainly have, Tom." The missionary rested for a moment on his elbow. "We've heard it come screaming in twice already. It lives in one of the upper apartments, I think." He nodded toward the Indian. "Manolo figured it out."

Tom drew in his breath sharply. "What's the answer, Uncle?"

"The Blue Devil built his treetop hideaway in the quietest spot he could find. You won't find any preacher monkeys or too many birds in this particular tree, that might give warning of his presence here. That eagle scares most creatures off. Clever, what?"

"The Blue Devil is as smart as the caciques, Uncle. He uses the eagle the way they use hornets' nests—to keep enemies off his premises. Clever, eh? Well, this time I'm really off to the races. See you soon."

"Good luck, Tom." The missionary and the Indian boy said it together.

A few minutes later Tom found himself back in the Blue Devil's private cabin. He wanted to look around for further clues, but there was no time for that now. He walked to the opening and took a firm hold on the liana cable. He felt a cold sweat breaking out on his forehead. The cable was quivering! Someone was coming up. The Blue Devil was returning. He was trapped! Tom took a quick look below. Sure enough. The Blue Devil was more than halfway up. He could see that he was carrying something.

Wild panic seized him. What could he do? Hurry back to the cabin where Uncle Leo and Manolo were? Mechanically he found himself fingering his bowie knife. It was such a temptation to cut the vine and send the Indian plunging down to his doom. But if he did that, their troubles would only be beginning. They had to find the *Paloma*, the *Paloma*— That was their first problem. They could come to grips with the Blue Devil later.

Tom's eyes frantically circled the room. It was ridiculous to think of hiding here. And there was no use crossing to the other cabin. His best bet was to climb up on the roof of this cabin. He leaned out and looked up. There were plenty of branches around the cabin. He grabbed one and hoisted himself up. He'd have to hurry. He had only seconds now.

He found himself several feet above the cabin. It was safer here, he figured. He strained his ears to listen. He could hear the Blue Devil now crawling near his cabin. A sound above him shot his head up.

It was the eagle shifting position in the biggest nest Tom had ever seen.

He felt as if he were between a sharp sword and a thick wall.

CHAPTER THIRTEEN

AN IMPORTANT FIND

Tom was careful not to make the slightest sound. It would be curtains, he told himself, if he was spotted by the eagle. It might scream a warning that would reveal his presence to the Blue Devil. For all he knew, the Blue Devil might be keeping the fierce-looking king of the skies as a sort of watchdog.

What was that the Indian had in his hand? Some tins of chipped beef! It meant he had just come from the *Paloma!* Tom felt like shouting, as dangerous as his predicament was. It sure was comforting to know the launch was anchored safely somewhere. It couldn't be too far away, because the Blue Devil hadn't been gone very long. So that's what the Blue Devil was up to. He'd keep the *Paloma* hidden until he disposed of his prisoners. Tom wondered whether he knew how to open the cans of beef, whether he had ever seen or used a can-opener. He probably knew more of the ways of white men than even his uncle suspected. No ordinary Indian, for example, would know how to pilot a launch like the *Paloma*.

Apparently the Blue Devil had known white men very well. He must have lived with them and learned much of their ways of life. Here he was, far from English-speaking people, yet he still spoke their tongue fluently and, indeed, seemed to speak it in preference to his native Indian dialect. This whole story about the Blue Devil was strange, Tom thought. Although he had gone back to his own people, he still lived and did many of the things a white man did. True the cabin was a dilapidated building but from all appearances this Indian preferred it to his tribal maloka or native house. He must have a knowledge of engines and of piloting a boat. He must know some of the uses of oil and, although he used the native bow and arrow, he must know something of the white man's weapons. Also he must enjoy the white man's food for he had taken some from the Paloma. This Indian was certainly a strange and unpredictable person to deal with.

Tom felt himself swaying on the bough. The wind was getting stronger.

He wanted to shift into a more comfortable position, but he didn't dare. If the Indian would only hurry and get out of there, so he could descend the liana cable and wait below for a chance to trail the Blue Devil back to the launch.

But here he was. Tom, poised like a stone statue, watched the Indian cross the vine bridge, hand over hand. What powerful, smooth strokes! He traveled faster than an ordinary person could walk. Tom breathed easier when he saw that the Indian was unarmed. It was clear that he had no immediate intention of killing Uncle Leo or Manolo. Tom started at the sound of wings fluttering above him. Panic gripped him when he saw the wing tips of the eagle. What if that strong-beaked bird pounced down on him? But there were several layers of branches between him and the aerie. Even an eagle would have trouble crashing through that barrier. He pulled himself nearer the trunk of the tree and watched, spellbound, as the eagle rose slowly from its massive nest that was made of twigs, sticks, and jungle grasses. He heard a confused screeching. There must be baby eagles in that nest. Tom gulped. Did this mother eagle have a mate, he wondered? But there was no time to worry about things like that now.

Tom lowered himself as quietly as he could to the next branch below. He kept stepping down until he was in position to slip into the cabin. A quick glance around told him the Blue Devil had left everything as it was. The tins of beef were on the floor beside the bundle of arrows. And beside them was a can-opener.

Tom wasted no more time. A few minutes later he was on the ground. A glance at his wrist watch told him it was a few minutes past two. He pushed his way through the foliage and walked slowly down

The Blue Devil Swung Across the Cable

the trail. He knew he had the chance of his life, now. He must be careful not to fumble it.

He stretched out on his back under a tree and rested his head on his clasped hands. He thought hard. Was it better to wait here for the Blue Devil to come down or to do a little private detective work while he was waiting? It might be hours before the Blue Devil came down. Tom leaped to his feet. It just occurred to him that the Indian had been perfectly dry when he came up the cable. It meant the *Paloma* was moored somewhere near the shore, or that the boat the Blue Devil used was on or near the riverbank. With a brief backward glance, Tom ran as fast as he could down the trail. He had almost reached the pier when he heard a sound that made his heart skip a beat. It was Ozzy, growling!

Tom shouted, wild with joy. Then he paused and strained to listen. The growling came from the left, through those waterfront growths just ahead. Tom unsheathed his machete and slashed a path through the damp vegetation.

"Ozzy, Ozzy," he called out to his pet, "I'll be right there."

There was a whimpering sound. Ozzy had recognized his voice. Tom pressed forward feverishly. A few minutes later he pushed through to the river's edge. He skirted the bank in the direction of the whimpering, and around the second bend he saw what he had been hoping and praying to see. The *Paloma,* moored just offshore!

And there on the deck waiting for him was the pet ocelot. How he got there, Tom had no idea, but one thing he did know was that he was more than glad to see him.

He jumped aboard and took the ocelot in his arms. He cuddled it while it licked his cheek. "Ozzy, you little idiot, how I love you." Tom put the ocelot down and examined the surplus oil tanks. They seemed intact. Now came the time for decision. His first thought was to hide some of the extra tanks in the bushes in case the Blue Devil should try any sabotage. Any Indian who had had so many dealings with oil engineers must know some of the things it was used for. But it might be a better plan to move the *Paloma* across the river and moor it in some hidden cove. He sank onto a seat and rested his face in his hands. This took some thought. If the Blue Devil found the launch missing, he might immediately rush back and murder Uncle Leo and Manolo.

"Oh, Uncle Leo, if only you and Manolo were here now," he whispered. He paced the deck frantically. But time was running out. He filled his canteen with water while he considered the best course of action. Whatever was done had to be done quickly. His eyes rested on the skiff. He could move the launch across the stream, row back, hide the skiff in the bushes, and rush back to the lookout tree. Then, the next time the Blue Devil headed downtrail, he could scale the liana cable, free his friends, and be ready for the next development. If all went well, the Blue Devil would be trapped. It was a chance he couldn't afford to miss.

Tom kept a vigilant eye on the path leading to the pier as he cruised across the river. He headed a couple of hundred yards back toward the entrance to the secret river and edged the bow into an inlet, where he secured it. Then he made sure everything was in order. He reached down to pat Ozzy, who was rubbing against his legs. "Sorry, pal, but you'll have to stay here now." He went below and poured some milk into a cup. "This will take care of you for a while, Ozzy."

Then Tom went below to refill his knapsack. There was no telling how long he would have to be away from the *Paloma* again. He had better prepare himself for a long stay. Then too Uncle Leo and Manolo would undoubtedly appreciate some more food. They had not thought they would be away from the boat so long.

In a few minutes he went topside again and looked cautiously about. No eyes seemed to be watching from the shore. Ozzy rubbed against him but Tom pushed him away gently. He climbed down into the skiff and rowed, with as little noise as possible, to the shore.

A short time later the skiff was grazing the pier. Tom hauled it ashore and pushed it into a clump of bushes. On his way up the trail leading to the lookout tower he had a snack to eat. He'd better get the nourishment while he could.

The late afternoon sun spun glints and shadows through the overhanging treetops. What a glorious day. All was so calm and so peaceful. "Like the lull before the storm," Tom whispered. Suddenly he drew back in horror. Ahead of him, slithering across the trail, was a huge speckled snake. He knew at a glance what it was. He had seen three of these whoppers in the zoo in Belem. An anaconda! The largest snake in Brazil—the largest in South America, in fact.

Tom whirled and rushed down trail. He knew that anacondas seldom if ever attacked humans, unless they were molested, but the thought of snakes was enough to give him the willies. He slowed down to a stop, panting. He had to husband his strength. There were liana cables to climb, maybe bridges to cross, and maybe a tussle with the powerful Blue Devil.

Tom spun around as a shadow flicked across his path. There, standing in the path, was the Blue Devil! Tom sprang into action. He rushed toward the Indian and tried to make a flying tackle. But the

Blue Devil was too quick for him. He danced back out of range. And his mocking laugh was the last thing Tom heard before he felt something crashing down on his head.

CHAPTER FOURTEEN

BETWEEN THE SWORD AND THE WALL

When Tom came back to his senses the missionary was bending over him. He pulled himself into a sitting position and glanced around numbly. His head was splitting from the worst headache he had ever had.

"Oh, Tom . . . Tom . . . you sure had me worried," the missionary said. "The Blue Devil must have given you a terrible wallop. There's a lump on your head the size of a tangerine." He helped him to his feet. "You've been out cold for several minutes. Feel okay now?"

Tom rubbed his head. He had no idea where he was or what he was doing. He put both hands to his head and tried to shake off his groggy feeling. Everything seemed to be whirling and swirling around.

"Tom, are you all right?" Mr. Jason put an arm around his shoulder to steady him.

Tom grinned. "Wow! What hit me, a sledge-hammer?"

"Well, my boy, you're lucky the Blue Devil hit you with his black-palm bow instead of piercing you with an arrow from it." He helped him to his feet.

Tom ran his eyes up the steepest cliff he had ever seen. There were spurs and crags and ledges at irregular intervals. How did he get here? The last thing he remembered was trying to tackle the Blue Devil on the hunters' trail. He looked questioningly at the missionary.

"I know what you're thinking, Tom." He handed him his canteen. "A drink of water won't do you any harm. Here."

Tom took a long drink. He felt nauseated and his throat felt parched. "Where's Manolo, Uncle Leo?" He waved in the direction of the cliff that was about ten yards in front of them. "How in the world did I get into this canyon? Why, I didn't even know there was a gorge like this around here." He looked at the wall of the cliff. It was worn smooth in too many places for them to scale it. "How do we get out of here, Uncle? And the Blue Devil—where is he?"

"Here, Tom, you'd better take a couple of aspirins, because you have a rugged job ahead of you." He looked up as it suddenly started to rain. "This rain will help us in one way, but it's liable to make the liana cable slippery, too. We've got to act fast and—"

Tom took the pills and washed them down with another swallow of water. "I feel as if I'm dreaming, Uncle. I don't get it. Just what happened? How did I get down here?"

The missionary glanced around furtively. "Let me fill in the gaps while you rest and regain your strength. After you left Manolo and me, the Blue Devil came in. He told us he planned to keep us prisoners until we told him where you were. He said the *Paloma* had been destroyed, and that we had no hope of escape."

"He was lying, Uncle. I found it and moored it across the river. It's—"

The frown disappeared from the missionary's face. "My prayers have been answered," he said gravely. "Thank God we still have the *Paloma*. But as I was saying, the moment he left, I made sure he had descended the liana cable leading down from his lookout tower. Then I crossed over and watched him head down the trail. I noticed he had his bow and arrow with him." The missionary sighed and mopped his brow. "You can imagine how I felt when I saw you coming up the trail. And just what I feared happened. You ran into him."

Tom shook his head disgustedly. "It was the anaconda I saw crossing the trail that threw me off. It kind of—well, I guess it knocked me off balance, and I got a little careless. Instead of watching where I was going, I ran right smack into that phantom. But then what happened?"

"I watched him sling you over his back and head back toward the lookout tower." The missionary kept glancing around nervously, as if he expected trouble. "You can imagine how I felt. I figured my best bet was to descend, so that if he took you up into the tower, one of us would be on the ground. My plan was to throw some pepper in his eyes as he passed me on the trail and then hit him over the head with the broadside of the machete. I've used a handful of pepper before, and it really works, I can tell you." He paused and turned his palms up. "It sure is sprinkling now."

"And so you came down from the tree." Tom was breathless with excitement. "And then what happened?"

"Well, much to my surprise, instead of heading for the lookout tower, the Blue Devil took a different trail. I knew he had no intention of lugging you up into the tower, so I trailed him. We walked about half a mile until he came to the brink of this precipice." Mr. Jason gestured toward the top of the cliff. "I was amazed, of course. I had no more idea than you that there was such a canyon around here." He shook his head. "I certainly couldn't see it from the lookout tower, but that's easy to understand, with all those trees in between."

"And then, Uncle?" Tom followed the missionary's gaze toward the jumble of trees behind them. "Why do you keep looking over there, Uncle?"

The missionary looked straight at Tom. "I don't

want to alarm you again, my boy, but I think there's a Motilon settlement back there. I could see smoke curling above the treetops from the top of this cliff." He glanced up, apprehensively, and jerked his thumb toward the top of the precipice. "The Blue Devil is up there, all tied up. I trailed him to the edge of the precipice while he was carrying you. Before I knew what he was up to, he disappeared over the edge of the cliff, with you slung over his shoulder. It takes a powerful man to—"

"Glad I was kayoed." Tom looked up and shuddered. "I would have been scared stiff if I knew anyone was carrying me over his shoulders as he shinnied down that liana cable. I don't see how he did it."

"Well, I waited until he came back up, then threw pepper into his eyes and walloped him over the head with my machete. He was knocked out cold. Then I tied him up the best I could. That's why we've got to hurry. We've got to get back up there and escape before he comes to and breaks his bonds."

"The Blue Devil up there and Motilons down here." Tom's voice was hollow. "We're between the sword and the wall for sure." He seized Mr. Jason's arm. "And Manolo? What about him?"

"He's still up there. Not in the cabin where you saw him, but in the lookout tower. He has orders to cut the liana cable if the Blue Devil tries to come up.

Manolo is safe temporarily, and he's keeping his eye peeled. We can always figure out a way later to get him down, even though we have to build some sort of ladder." He slung his knapsack over his shoulder. "And now, Tom, we've got to hurry. I'm going to haul myself up the cable first. I don't trust the Blue Devil. There's a chance that he's up there lying in wait, and I wouldn't put anything past him. He might use some of our strategy and cut the cable. As I say, I tied him up, but you never know how easy it is for these Indians to wriggle out of bonds."

Tom crooked his arms and yawned. "I may seem bored, Uncle, but I'm just bushed. And it looks like a long haul up there."

"And that's what's been worrying me, Tom. Do you think you can make it?"

Tom shot a glance up the wet, slippery precipice. "I *have* to make it, Uncle. I feel much stronger now, anyway." He stroked his chin and tried to appear cheerful. "Let's put the show on the road, Uncle." He glanced at his watch. Exactly four-thirty. Rain was pouring down, and the sky was dark gray. It was somber and depressing, but if luck was with them they'd be able to escape. He glanced behind them.

From all he could see there was no sign of village. These people had learned to live in hiding like the animals of the forest. Only the smoke from their cook fires told the presence of a settlement. And now even that could not be seen through the murky atmosphere. If Mr. Jason had not seen the smoke, Tom would have no idea that it existed.

Tom wondered if the Motilons knew he was there at the bottom of the cliff. It was possible that they had scouts out on all sides of their village. Had the Blue Devil told them of him and his uncle and Manolo? Was the Blue Devil their chief? How powerful was he with his own people? All these questions went through Tom's head as he stood there, and all went unanswered for the time being.

"The smoke came from a spot about three hundred yards back there, Tom." The missionary stooped to tie his shoelace. "Just remember that. Even if we don't get anything out of this mission, we at least know where some of the Motilons live. And maybe we can capture the Blue Devil and take him back to Belem. I've given up all hope of making a Christian out of that fellow, after all my talks with him. I fear he is at best a black-hearted pagan."

Tom followed at a brisk trot through the foliage fringing the precipice. The rain was beating a steady tattoo, but he was used to being soaked to the skin. No sign now of the gaily colored birds he had seen earlier in the day. He flung a worried look over his shoulder now and then, as if he expected to see some Motilons sneaking up behind them.

By the time they reached the cliff, his feeling of

dread was more intense. He clenched his hands and looked up the wall of the dripping cliff. It would be tough going. One slip and—

He kicked a stone into the underbrush and watched his uncle grab hold of the stout vine. What would these Indians do without vines, he asked himself. He found it hard to concentrate on what his uncle was saying. "Look, Tom, I'll give you the signal to come up by jerking the vine three times. Like this. So keep your eyes peeled. With those Indians back there, it's best not to do any shouting. Okay?"

"Okay, Uncle. Good luck." The words almost stuck in Tom's throat. He didn't move a muscle until Mr. Jason disappeared in the murk about forty feet up. He wiped the tears of worry from his eyes with the back of his hand. Uncle Leo was taking an awful chance, and he was so casual about it.

He paced back and forth. He felt chilly and uncomfortable in his sopping khaki clothes. He whirled every time some jungle creature scampered through the brush. Each time he was sure it would be a Motilon. If they came up now—

He strained to catch some sound of the missionary. He could hear nothing but the patter of rain driving in on the cliff. The movement of the cable told him, however, that his uncle was still hanging on. Tom dared not look away. His feelings were jumbled,

"I'll Signal When I Get to the Top."

his nerves jangled. He kept on telling himself it was like being trapped between a sword and a wall. The Blue Devil might be ready and waiting up at the other end of the rope. There were other Motilons back there in the jungle, too close for comfort. He shot another glance toward the Indian settlement.

How far up the cliff was his uncle? Had he found a ledge on which to rest? How much farther had he to go? Tom flexed his knees and threw his arms over his head. How soon would he have to start his hand-over-hand journey?

Tom gasped. The cable was still now. He checked his wrist watch to see how long his uncle had been climbing. It seemed like hours, but it was only eight minutes. Surely he couldn't have made it so soon. He must be resting on one of the rocky shelves. At least, Uncle Leo had not signaled by jerking the rope up and down three times. He couldn't have done it in the brief time Tom had taken his eyes off the cable. Or could he? His nervous gaze switched once more to the underbrush. It was impossible to see more than ten or fifteen yards in the dusk. They could rush out of that underbrush and pounce on him before he knew it. If they did rush him, his best bet would be to start shinnying up the rope. He wished he had some weapon besides a machete. He glanced at the boulders lying around. He picked one up and bounced it off a tree. Maybe that fast ball he used to throw at opposing batters when he pitched for his high-school team would come in handy now. He jumped. The rope was swaying a little again. Uncle Leo was on his way!

Tom stood there in the driving rain, clenching his hands. He felt chilled now—chilled on a July day that had begun by being so hot. What about the Blue Devil up there? Was he still waiting in this rain? Suppose he had taken shelter under a tree, or something, and was waiting in hiding for Uncle Leo? In that case, it would be curtains for Uncle Leo, for him, for Manolo and Ozzy—for their whole party.

He drew a gloomy mental picture of Uncle Leo crawling over the edge of the cliff and finding the Blue Devil waiting with an arrow pointed at the missionary. And even if he wasn't there, it would be dangerous. He might be waiting farther down the trail where he would be least expected. Tom kicked a stone against the cliff. There was no use getting so gloomy about everything.

The cable was still twitching. "Hurry, hurry, hurry, Uncle," he whispered. Time was running out on them. Uncle Leo had been climbing for almost twenty minutes now. Tom shifted a startled look over toward the brush where he swore something had just moved. Maybe some animal. It could have been a capybara or an onca or a little honey bear, even. Tom could feel his Adam's apple moving up and down.

He looked back at the cable. It had stopped moving. Maybe Uncle Leo was crawling over the side, now. Tom kept his eyes fixed on the cable. All he wanted was to see it jerked three times. Why, oh why, didn't Uncle Leo give the signal?

Tom whirled, terrified. No question about it. He saw a copper form, then another glide through the bushes. Maybe they hadn't noticed him in the dark, and were more careless than usual. Tom picked up several boulders, shot a glance at the rope. Still no signal. He moistened his lips and stood like a statue. He heard the crackling sound of a twig breaking, thought he saw a branch being thrust aside, as if someone was cautiously peering through. He could stand the suspense no longer. He wound up and cannon-balled a boulder into the bushes. He heard a scream of rage, a scream that sent tremors down his spine. The Motilons were on the loose.

He fired three more stones, then stood there as if paralyzed. Two Indians came charging toward him, yelling blue murder. What a horrible language! Neither was armed. Tom leaped high into the air, grabbed the cable and began to haul himself up in a burst of energy. He dared not look down, but he could hear the snarling Indians. He hunched up his shoulders and climbed frantically, already panting from the exertion. He winced when a boulder bounced off the wall of the cliff a few feet above him.

And now he could feel the cable become taut. It meant only one thing. One of the Indians was going to climb up behind him. It would be a race to the death. And even if he won the race, what would be waiting up there at the other end of the rope?

CHAPTER FIFTEEN

PURSUIT

Tom heard the Motilon on the ground yelling. He was probably calling for a third Motilon to come with a bow and arrow. He probably figured he didn't have time to go back and get any weapons himself. Tom ducked as another boulder bounced off the wall.

So that was it! One of the Indians was trying to slow him down or knock him down while the other pursued him up the rope! Tom inched upward as fast as he could, expecting at any moment to be struck by a stone. Disaster threatened from every side. The cable might break with the weight of two persons—maybe three persons, for he wasn't sure Uncle Leo had reached the top of the cliff—on it. Tom wished he could understand what the Indian on the ground was saying.

He struggled to keep his wits about him, winced as a small stone stung him on the leg. Another glanced off his shoulder, and that one hurt like fury. He held on grimly and paused momentarily when he felt himself slipping down the cable. He shot a terrified look down at the Indian's powerful arms, that were working like pistons. Tom could hear him grunting.

Tom buckled and almost lost his grip when a large stone bounced off his back. It seemed the higher he got, the better the Motilon's aim was. He closed his eyes and held on, clenching his teeth as he whispered a prayer. The pain was piercing, and it sapped his strength. He could see the Indian, now, less than ten feet below him. The ground was swallowed up in the mist, but he knew he must be around fifteen yards up. Just above he saw a shelf. His best chance was to stop there and try to kick the Indian down the cable. The Indian on the ground was still heaving stones, but his aim was getting wilder now, thank goodness.

Tom could feel beads of cold perspiration on his forehead, and his arms were aching. He swung onto the shelf and gripped the cable and waited. He had the advantage of being above the Indian. That murderous savage was going to have a battle on his hands. He was not as husky as the Blue Devil, but at that he was fifteen or twenty pounds heavier than Tom. He felt as though he were in a trance when the top of the Indian's head loomed out of the fog. In about three seconds—

Tom jackknifed his legs and came down hard on the Motilon's hands. He felt those hands slide down, lose their grip momentarily, but the Indian did not fall. Tom could see he was holding on with one hand while he shook his fist defiantly with the other. He made no outcry.

Tom stiffened with horror. For the first time he saw that the Indian had a knife between his teeth. He had not noticed it before. He must have been carrying it in his belt. Tom kicked away savagely, and once more that powerful hand lost its hold. Tom waited for him to climb another foot or so, then lashed out again, letting himself slide down while he kicked as hard as he could with both feet. Then he clambered back onto the shelf and tried to recover his breath. His chest felt sore from his heavy breathing. He had barely stepped onto the shelf when the knife clattered off the cliff wall just before him. That had been a narrow squeak—a battle to the death, and no mistake. He waited tensely for the Indian's next move. Here he was now. Thank heavens he no longer had his knife, anyhow—

Tom decided to discourage him once and for all. He let himself slide down as fast as possible, gained momentum as he went, and fell heavily against the Indian's hands. He landed with both feet on the Indian's shoulders, kicked away as the savage tried to grab his legs. Then he heard the Indian shriek as he lost his grip and plummeted to the ground. For one tense moment Tom thought the fall had killed him. He felt as though he had murdered somebody, even though he had no other choice. But then he heard the two Indians angrily muttering. The one who had fallen was clearly not hurt.

The rain still fell in torrents. Tom could not see what was happening on the ground. He could see nothing above him but the slippery vine cable, the murky half-darkness and the wall of wet rock. He scrambled up the liana rope quickly to get out of the reach of the maddened Motilons. What would they do now? Would the other one clamber up the cable after him? With their greater experience they could climb much faster and with more assurance than he. Then too it was a help to know where you were going and what you might expect to find at the top of the vine. Here these natives had a decided advantage over Tom.

With a burst of speed bred from necessity, Tom sped up the cable. No one came after him immediately. He could feel the cable swinging free behind him. He pulled himself up another few feet. The wet vine slipped in his hands and he found he was not making as rapid progress up the liana cable as he had hoped.

A few feet farther and Tom came to a narrow ledge. He stopped to get his breath and to wipe the moisture from his hands. Down below he could hear the natives talking loudly as though in anger. Were there some newcomers? Had they received reinforcements from the village?

In the midst of terrible danger Tom forced himself to think. Past adventures had developed in him the explorer's ability to plan the next move while his body met the physical challenge of the moment. He keyed himself now for what might be ahead. "One-a, two-a, three-a, four-a," he counted. The sound of his own voice seemed to give him courage. His body responded to the regular rhythm and he found that his movements were becoming smoother and more powerful as he found his second wind. His hands were no longer slipping on the wet liana vine.

Tom shot up the cable rapidly and with renewed hope. He was making good progress now. He wondered about their next move. What was going on above? Maybe Uncle Leo had been trying to signal him, but with all that weight on the cable, it would have been impossible. Tom hunched up his shoulders when another shower of small stones hit the cliff wall. One stone glanced back off the top of his head. Both Indians were throwing at once, he judged. And then it happened. An arrow whizzed past him and bounced off the cliff. Reinforcements had arrived. Stones were bouncing all around now, and here was a second arrow. He was too high up now, shrouded in the murk and the mist, for them to take accurate aim. But one lucky hit from a black-palm arrow and that would be the end of Tom Stetson. Tom tried to keep calm as he redoubled his efforts. In another thirty feet or so he would again be able to rest on a ledge. He kept going even when a stone caught him smack on the leg. The arrows were falling short.

He felt safer when the stones began to carom off the wall beneath him. But now his breath was coming in short gasps, and the cable was getting harder and harder to hold. His hands were slipping like automobile tires ascending an icy hill. It was the worst jam he had ever been in. Hockey and football —what child's play by comparison. He'd have to rest soon, have to rest soon . . . he felt dizzy and sick to his stomach. He shuddered. Something was happening to the cable! He felt himself being pulled out into space, farther and farther from the wall. "No, no!" he shouted. It was terrifying to be shaken around like this, not knowing where you were going to fall, or what you'd crash into. He knew what was going on—the Indians were trying to dislodge him, make him lose his grip!

What a fool he had been! Why hadn't he pulled the bottom end of the cable up with him? It was heavy, but why couldn't he have tied it around his waist? Of course he couldn't have. It was too heavy and too bulky. He was losing his mind. But maybe he could have cut off the bottom part. But it was too late to think of any of those things now. A fall from here would be fatal, he was sure. It might as well be. If he were alive when he landed, he wouldn't be alive very long.

He held on grimly, his head hunched between his shoulders, trying to preserve his last bit of strength. The Indians were still snapping him from side to side, trying to shake him loose. It was almost impossible to shinny up the way he was being buffeted around. If he could keep from sliding all the way down, he'd be lucky.

And that ominous silence above didn't help matters. It looked more and more like a hopeless struggle. Surely Uncle Leo would have somehow let him know if he was up there. He certainly must have heard the commotion below him. Or did he find the Blue Devil waiting for him when he reached the top of the cliff?

The Indians must have let go. Tom felt himself swinging like a pendulum back toward the jagged wall. He spun around and around, extending his legs in an effort to protect himself. It didn't work. He crashed heavily, his right shoulder hitting the wall. For an instant his right hand lost all its strength, and his arm felt numb. He barely managed to hold on with his left hand. The impact had knocked most of the breath he had left out of him. He couldn't stand much more.

He hung there limp and tortured with anxiety.

Tom Swung Toward the Jagged Wall

The cards were stacked against him, all right. There they were, the fiends, pulling him away from the wall. The murderous tribe would keep this up until he fell off. Inhuman beings! Wild savages! And Uncle Leo thought he could civilize them! Tom marshaled every ounce of his strength and tried to climb a few more feet. The higher he got, the less they would be able to drag him from the wall, he told himself. He spun around dizzily, but he held on, even though his head was reeling, spinning. He was fifteen, maybe twenty feet from the wall, and they were still pulling. He went up a bit more and out, then felt himself whirling back toward the wall. What if he smashed into one of those spurs? In the dusk he could hardly see where he was going, but now he could see the dark wall falling in toward him. He spread his legs wide and hit the wall feet first.

He wasted no time. He began to climb furiously. "One-a, two-a," he grunted, pulling hand over hand. This method of counting cadence somehow seemed to help. "Three-a, four-a," he continued. The sound of his voice reassured him, made him forget he was alone. It ended the unfriendly silence that was broken only by the patter of the rain. He ascended another ten feet and stepped wearily onto a shelf just before they tugged on the cable for a third time. He braced himself, teetering precariously on the edge of the shelf for a moment. There was enough room to sit down, thank goodness. He lowered himself cautiously when he noticed that the shelf sloped downward. And it was wet and slippery with the rain. He leaned back and rubbed his forehead, waited for the rope to swing back.

He heard it before he saw it, and the second it came within reach he clutched at it. He would rest a few more minutes. He closed his eyes and settled back, his chest heaving. Suddenly he screamed as he felt himself being pulled off the ledge. He released his grip on the cable just in time, kept himself from slipping by bracing himself with his feet, and again drew back against the wall, in fear and trembling. He was too stunned at first to realize how close he had come to falling. And he was about two-thirds of the way up, now. The fall would surely have killed him, and no mistake.

"Steady, Tom," he whispered hoarsely. "You'll still make it if you keep cool." He heard the cable whipping back toward him.

He reached out into the rain and missed it. It hadn't fallen back in the same place! Tom broke out into a cold sweat. It must have caught on one of the spurs. He drew in his breath sharply. He pictured himself being stranded on the shelf. He might stay there for days yelling for help that might never come.

He groped frantically for the cable. He had to use

his right hand, because it seemed safer to lie on his back and steady himself by pushing on a spur with his right leg. But what an awkward position it was! He couldn't reach the cable. Where was it? He moved nearer the edge of the shelf and felt around the corner of the ledge. He could barely touch it with his fingertips. And hurry, hurry, hurry before those fiends pulled it away again, and careful, careful, because if they jerked it while he had a firm grip on it— He shifted position and inched as close to the edge as he dared. He wrapped his fingers around the cable and tried to pull it toward him. It was pulled tight. One of the Indians must be climbing again!

Tom bit his lip. One jam after another. He couldn't pull the cable back off the spur, and it was hard to grab in the position he was in. It would be dangerous to turn over and reach for the cable with his left hand. Yet he had to do something. And quick!

But what? He tried to shake off his despair and exhaustion. He felt almost paralyzed. He heard the cable rustling and swishing in his wet grip. He dared not let go, because the weight on it might pull it beyond his reach, and then he would be sunk for sure.

There was only one—maybe two—things he could do. He could hold on firmly with his right hand

and ease himself down off the shelf so he could grab
the cable with his left, but that was terribly dangerous. The alternative was to warn whoever was climbing to go back down before he cut it. But if he did
that, suppose the other Indian pulled the cable out
of his grip? It was too much of a chance to take. And
besides, come to think of it, he couldn't threaten
these Motilons, because they wouldn't understand
him.

He took a deep breath, strengthened the grip of
his right hand and swung down off the shelf, reaching out with his left hand. He slid down a couple of
feet as he took hold and quickly flicked over his
right wrist. Then he hauled himself back up and
stepped onto the shelf.

He stood erect, balancing himself. After taking
a few deep breaths, he began to climb vigorously. He
felt he was nearing the top now. He kept moving. It
was farther up than he had suspected. He stopped on
another shelf to rest. He was careful this time to keep
a firm grip on the cable. He could feel his pulse
racing. When it quieted down a little he began the
weary climb, the homestretch. His strength was once
more failing, but the prospect of reaching the top
spurred him on. His legs, wound around the cable,
told him the cable was hanging free. He felt relieved,
but only for a moment. There were still plenty of
problems left when he got to the top.

Another ghastly thought came into his mind. Suppose the Blue Devil had put Uncle Leo out of commission and was waiting for him to get to the top. And then cut the cable— But no, no, Tom told himself. The Blue Devil wouldn't cut his own stairway. It might be the only way to his settlement. But was it? One gloomy thought after another filled his mind as he climbed upward.

The cable grew taut again. What—what were those Indians below up to now? He paused, frozen with horror. They were tugging the vine back and forth now. They were trying to wear it away against some sharp ledge that would bite into it. Tom flew into a panic. He poked against the cliffside looking for another shelf. Here was one. He stepped onto it and whipped his machete from his belt. He cut the cable. Too bad, in a way. It was the only known way of getting to the Motilon settlement. But as far as Tom was concerned, he never wanted to get any closer to these mysterious savages than he had already been. He looked up, saw the brow of the cliff in the wet dusk.

He shinnied up fast, husbanding his last ounce of strength. He stopped just under the edge of the cliff. He could hear nothing. He dared not call for his uncle.

Cautiously he pulled himself over the rim of the precipice and crawled up the grassy slope. It felt so wonderful to be on firm ground again. He crept into a clump of bushes and lay flat on his stomach. He could see nothing, hear nothing. There was not a sign of Uncle Leo or of the Blue Devil.

CHAPTER SIXTEEN

SURROUNDED BY MOTILONS

Tom lay on the ground for a moment, not daring to move a muscle. He had a choking sensation as he tried to imagine what had happened to Uncle Leo. Somehow the Blue Devil must have untied himself. And then what? Had he waited up here for the missionary, and where were they both now?

Tom crawled on his stomach toward the shrub where the liana cable's end was still tied. Dusk had fallen, and the dismal rain was still beating down. Tom could scarcely see, but he saw enough to tell him that the bushes near by looked trampled. There had been a struggle, all right. He stepped on something solid. Uncle Leo's binoculars! The strap was broken. Had the glasses been torn off during a scuffle? Tom looked down over the edge of the cliff and shuddered. No, no—Uncle Leo couldn't have been pushed over. He couldn't, he just couldn't. Tom dabbed at the tears that were streaming down his cheek as he glanced wildly around in the cold, forbidding bleakness. He put the binoculars in his knapsack and probed through the thicket to see if there was any other evidence. In the mud near the edge of the cliff he saw footprints, but it was impossible to tell whose they were. The rain had smudged them. But a struggle had taken place near the very brink of the precipice. No doubt of that!

Tom moistened his lips and stood there, undecided what to do. He had a hollow feeling inside. The Blue Devil must have already murdered Uncle Leo. He wiped away a tear with the back of his hand. Nobody had ever been kinder to him. And here he was alone in the dark, rain-soaked jungle, being hunted, perhaps, by wild savages who were determined to kill him. A terrible feeling of loneliness and despair swept over him. It was so dark he could barely make out the blur of the overhanging trees.

He thought of Manolo in the treetop cabin. Maybe Manolo would know something about Uncle Leo. Maybe the Blue Devil had drugged his uncle again and now had him tied up in the cabin with Manolo. Maybe, maybe, maybe— Tom kicked a stone over the precipice. He was so sick of not knowing what was going on.

Tom looked around for something to give him direction. Where was he? In what direction did the cabin and the lookout lie? He had no idea how the Blue Devil had taken him to the foot of the cliff. This thought brought back the fact that he had been hit over the head with the Indian's huge black-palm bow. Funny, in his haste to get away from the Motilons he had completely forgotten that his head was sore. Carefully, he passed his hand over his head. Yes, there was the bump as big as a tangerine, just as his uncle had said. But Tom had no time to worry about the bump now. He had to get away from this place and find his friend Manolo before he met the Blue Devil again.

The rain had stopped and the clouds were breaking. The air was clearer and Tom could see some distance on all sides. He stood still, looking about for some familiar landmark. It should be possible to see the tall tree and the eagle's nest from some distance. There was a tall tree. But was it the right one? Tom squinted his eyes trying to see better in the half-light. Then overhead came the scream of an eagle and the huge bird flew overhead directly toward the tall tree Tom had spotted.

He looked up wonderingly as the moon glimmered through the treetops. Even that faint light was comforting. He fingered his flashlight as he walked toward the lookout tower. In spite of the darkness, he walked cautiously. He knew almost nothing about the habits of these Motilons. They might have some other way of climbing up the cliff. He halted in front of the bush that hid the bottom of the tremendous tree. He pushed aside the branches and pushed his way through, taking care to shield his face from the briers. How the Blue Devil managed to get through this stuff without getting all scratched up still mystified him. He paused, and hearing nothing but the whirring of some night insects, pushed open the false panel and groped his way through the black-as-night tunnel. It was all so frightening. He thought of the blood-lapping bats he had read about, with their sharp teeth that they used to gouge their victims. He shook off the gruesome thought and started up the liana cable. He had recovered his strength now, and he was scarcely breathing hard when he jumped into the lookout tower. Complete silence. He wanted to turn on his flashlight, but he didn't dare. He wanted to call to Manolo, too, but it was too dangerous. He stooped down and grabbed the cable that led to the other treetop cabin. It was so slippery! He told himself to be extra careful. One false move and—

He was almost half across the bridge when a terrible scream rent the air. He was so terrified and startled he almost lost his grip. He heard an ominous fluttering of wings. It was the eagle, swooping down. Tom hung on grimly, terror in his heart. He imagined the eagle lunging at him with those sharp, powerful talons, and its curved beak. He could hear the eaglets screeching in the nest just above him. Should he go back or press forward? He could see, dimly outlined in the moonlight, the spreading branches beneath him. If the eagle came too close, he told himself he would let go his hold and hope he could grab one of the branches on the way down. And then, what? The lowest branches were so high above the ground— The Blue Devil had seen to that. He had cut the lower branches to prevent any mass attack on his aerial retreat.

In the dim light Tom saw the eagle glide into its nest. He breathed a deep sigh of relief as he hurried across to the cabin. A moment later he felt like cheering. He could see Manolo on the floor curled up in sleep.

He hopped into the cabin and bent over his little friend. "Manolo, wake up." He shook the Indian boy and felt him stir.

"Tom. It is you." Manolo wearily pulled himself up. "And Mr. Jason?"

Tom bit his lip. The way Manolo mentioned his uncle's name brought back all the dread he had felt.

"I—I don't know, Manolo. I have no idea where he is." He paused and sobbed. "There's no time now to tell you what's happened. We—we'd better get out of here for now and go back to the *Paloma*. There's nothing we can possibly do tonight."

Manolo put his arm around Tom's shoulder and pressed him close. "Do not worry, Tom. Mr. Jason is too smart. Even Blue Devil will find out that."

Tom felt comforted. It was one of the longest speeches he had ever heard Manolo make. He smiled

The Eagle Swooped Down

through his tears.

"I hope you're—right, Manolo." He could say no more.

A few minutes later Tom, closely followed by Manolo, was descending the liana vine from the lookout cabin. Neither of them breathed even a whisper. Tom listened intently as he waited for the little Indian to join him in the tunnel. He reached out and helped him find the opening to the tunnel.

"Okay, Manolo, let's go. Our next stop is the *Paloma*. Do you feel all right?"

"All except water," Manolo said. "Much rain all day, but much sleep, too, so I do not catch in my hand much water."

Tom handed him his canteen without a word and waited while he drank. As tired and thirsty as Manolo was, he noticed, he drank slowly.

"All right, Manolo. Let's take it easy now," he said. He led the way through the bushes and a moment later they were on the open trail leading down to the pier. All Tom could think of as they slogged along through the sopping wet underbrush that bordered the trail was the anaconda he had seen before. On any camping trip he had taken he could use his flashlight, but here he had to be careful to keep from being seen or heard. He glanced over his shoulder. Manolo was just a few steps behind him, but he was gliding along so noiselessly Tom hardly knew he was there.

Tom glanced up at the stars. The storm clouds had lifted now, and the moon that was almost full made it much easier to see where they were going. Tom halted, startled, when what looked like a huge rat scampered across the trail. It was nothing but a capybara, probably, he told himself. A moment later he froze again in his tracks. He was sure he heard the sound of a jungle telephone. He had heard that ominous sound before. The Indians of the Amazon wilderness sometimes relayed messages to one another by striking an ironwood tree. The resulting sound could be heard for long distances.

Tom turned to consult with Manolo. "Did you hear anything just now?" he asked.

Manolo nodded gravely. "Come from behind us," he whispered. "It is message for someone far down near river."

"The hunt is on," Tom whispered. He wet his lips and glanced back over his shoulder. "Somehow those Motilons have come up the cliff without using the liana vine I cut." He thought hard for a moment. "Do you think they searched in the treetop cabin and discovered you were missing, Manolo?"

The little Indian shrugged. "Hard to fool Motilons," he said simply.

Dawn broke suddenly. Tom felt as though they were being watched by those murderous eyes of the

Motilons from behind the wall of underbrush. It was such a helpless feeling to be pitted unarmed against a ghostly enemy which you could not hear and could almost never see.

He clutched at Manolo's arm. "Let's make a dash for it. Those fiends can't be far behind us now."

Tom raced down the trail, with Manolo just a few steps behind. He had almost reached the pier when he heard Manolo's whisper.

"Look, Tom." Manolo was pointing to a place in the path where the jungle grass had been trampled so much only the soft wet ground remained. And in the mud he could see the footprints that had been made by two persons. One person was barefoot, the other wore heavy duty shoes. Who else but the Blue Devil and Uncle Leo could have left these footprints?

Tom stared wild-eyed at Manolo.

Manolo was smiling and nodding vigorously at the same time. "Mr. Jason is alive up to here anyway," he said cautiously. He studied the footprints again. "He walk ahead and man without shoes walk just behind."

"Thank heavens Uncle Leo is all right," Tom whispered. "But where can he and the Blue Devil—?"

He was interrupted by what sounded like another gong. The tone was low and could just be heard. This time it came from the other side of the river.

Someone was relaying a message back to the Motilons behind them. And it wasn't hard to guess who it was. It was the Blue Devil! He was lord of his domain all right. He could see everything that was going on from his lookout tower and communicate with his people by striking those ironwood trees.

Tom gestured for Manolo to follow and ducked into the underbrush leading to the place where he had hidden the skiff. His mind was working fast. If the Blue Devil and Uncle Leo were on the other side of the river, how had they crossed? He knew the Motilons must have canoes of some kind, but so far he had seen no sign of any.

Another gong, then another and still another. A series of sounds, now louder and clearer, were coming from all sides. Tom stopped to listen. He felt sick to his stomach. They were being hemmed in on all sides. He whirled. Another single low tone, closely followed by three shorter sounds came from the opposite side of the river. The Blue Devil must be giving instructions of some kind.

"Have you any idea what message they are trying to send?" Tom asked.

But the little Indian boy shook his head. "Message secret. Only Motilons know."

"Come on, Manolo." Tom pushed through the thick underbrush, paying no attention to the thorns. A few minutes later he broke out into the open spot.

For an instant he felt like jumping up and down with joy. The skiff was there. Yes, the skiff was there—but the oars were gone. And tied around one of the oarlocks was a piece of blue ribbon!

CHAPTER SEVENTEEN

THE DUGOUT ARMADA

Tom paled. He listened stupefied to the jungle telephone signals. They were coming closer. *Doom, doom,* they seemed to be saying, instead of *boom, boom.* It was like the ominous beating of the tom-toms that in some parts of the world, meant approaching death. That was on the Island of Haiti, he remembered numbly, as his glance was riveted on the blue ribbon that was a mocking reminder that the Blue Devil was closing in on him.

"This looks bad, Manolo." Tom rested his hands on his hips and looked into the little Indian's eyes. There was no fear there, but there was no merriment, either. He could tell that Manolo was fully aware of the tight spot they were in.

Manolo gestured toward the skiff. "Too dangerous to row in boat, even with oars," he said quietly. "Motilons wait on other side and can see."

Tom, dazed, rubbed his brow. "I know, Manolo, I know that too well." He waved toward the underbrush. "There are Motilons back in there and on all sides of us. No matter what we do, we're in for it." He kicked up a piece of turf. "If only we could somehow get across to the *Paloma*."

Manolo folded his arms and bowed his head. "One thing only to do, Tom. We swim under water. That is best."

Tom's jaw sagged. "Swim under—water? In that water, Manolo?" He shook his head vigorously. "Not me. Why, that dirty river is full of piranhas and electric eels and heaven knows what else." He screened his eyes and looked toward the opposite bank. "And besides, I don't think I could swim all the way across under water."

Manolo was nodding. "It is far swim. And it is full of danger." He waved toward their surroundings without turning his head. "But here is danger, too. More danger." A hard glint came into his eyes. "I trust piranha and eel more than Blue Devil and tribe."

For a moment Tom half forgot their dangerous predicament. It was so unusual for Manolo to talk to such an extent. In spite of his outward calm, Manolo was worried—more worried than Tom had ever seen him before.

Tom paced back and forth as the jungle signals were relayed across the water. It was all so unreal. The hunter running down the hunted, coming closer all the time! He wondered whether the Indians knew where they were hiding at this moment. If his imagination could be trusted, they knew, because they seemed to be closing in on them. It seemed as though a gigantic net was about to cover them. Something had to be done.

The dark river, the electric eels, the piranhas, and probably alligators, the savages skilled in using huge black-palm bows and arrows, and—the Blue Devil himself. All these things stood against them. And that was not counting the treacherous jungle itself and their unfamiliarity with the country and now —the jungle telephone booming back and forth!

But Tom knew that counting only the circumstances against them would not rescue them from their predicament. He thought, too, of the things in their favor. First, there was Manolo. He knew the ways of the jungle and he was level-headed. Then they each had their machetes—and weeks in the jungle had taught Tom to use the weapon with skill and confidence. He fingered it in the darkness, taking strength from the cold steel.

Tom thrust the branches aside and measured the distance across the secret river. He shuddered. He kept thinking of those razor-sharp teeth of the river gangsters, the piranhas. If Manolo and he only had weapons of some kind. While he stood there, bewildered, he rummaged around in his knapsack, as if he hoped to find some weapon he had forgotten. Both he and Manolo had bowie knives, as well as machetes but that was all. And what good were bowie knives against these terrible enemies, who had those long black-palm bows and arrows?

He stepped back abruptly. "Did you hear that, Manolo?" He waited tensely as Manolo nodded.

"Someone in boat on river." There was a note of excitement in Manolo's voice. "Come this way, I think."

Tom swallowed. Slowly he parted the branches and peered through. A huge dugout canoe—it was thirty feet long at least—was gliding down the river toward them. In it, with black bows slung over their backs, were eleven Motilons.

Tom gasped. "Look, Manolo," he whispered. "They're coming directly toward us."

Manolo crept forward past Tom and looked. His gaze followed the dugout canoe, then shifted at the sound of something coming from the opposite direction.

"Two boats," he said, without a trace of emotion.

"There are eleven Indians in the other canoe, too," Tom whispered. "We're sunk."

A moment later the first canoe he had seen glided right past them. Tom breathed a sigh of relief. "They don't seem to know where we are, Manolo." And it suddenly occurred to him that the jungle telephone signals had ceased.

"They are searching now, Tom." Manolo rubbed his chin thoughtfully. "We must make no noise.

Wait to see what happen."

Tom's fingers rested on the can of black pepper in his knapsack. He pulled it out and balanced it in his hand.

"Look, Tom. Third dugout. In it only one Motilon. Now comes more. Many canoes, and all with one Motilon only."

Tom stared, spellbound. There was a regular fleet of dugouts. These were much smaller—not more than ten or twelve feet long. They seemed to be patrolling the river. "Thirteen, fourteen, fifteen," he counted to himself. And he saw more of them scattered at various points on the river. It was one of the strangest sights he had ever seen. A kind of Indian navy on the prowl—a flotilla, looking for two boys.

"I wonder what would happen if we started pounding one of those ironwood trees, Manolo," Tom whispered excitedly. "Maybe it would get them all mixed up and—"

Manolo shook his head as he bent forward to watch the canoes. "No good. Help them find us quicker only," he said.

A sudden idea struck Tom. It was too fantastic, he told himself. But anything was worth a try, now, with the fix they were in. He thought hard as he mopped his brow. The morning sun blazed down through the sheltering foliage, but Tom knew that it was liable to rain any moment in this part of the tropics. There was seldom much warning.

This was one time Tom hoped it would rain and rain soon. Rain now would help to hide Manolo and himself. It would cool the jungle and let them breathe. But there was not a cloud in the sky.

"Say, Manolo." He nudged the little Indian in the ribs. "You remember Uncle Leo saying that when these Motilons are hurt they never cry out? He said that if they hollered, it was probably because they were angry, not hurt."

Manolo nodded as he kept his eyes glued on the dozens of dugouts that were crisscrossing up and down the river. He said nothing.

"If we batted one of these Motilons over the head with a club or something as he came by, you don't think he would scream out, do you?"

A puzzled look had crept into Manolo's face. "Motilons too proud to yell when hurt," he said. "Only cowards yell when hurt."

Tom's eyes narrowed as he nodded his agreement. He was watching the Motilon who was now heading in their direction. "But they might shout out a warning," he said.

Manolo shrugged. "Maybe shout warning," he said. "But if we hit hard enough he cannot shout warning, either." He looked up toward the sky. "Or if macaws squawk or preacher monkeys make noise it is hard to hear."

They Saw the Indians Pass in Small Dugouts

Tom's gaze followed his toward a near-by treetop. There was something in the way Manolo spoke that made him look. There, on a branch, were three preacher monkeys. It was clear that they had not noticed their presence. If those monkeys had, they would be yammering for them to get away.

"By gosh, Manolo, here is our golden opportunity. Let's get those preachers up there to start a noisy sermon, then we'll wham this Motilon who's heading for us. We'll knock him out, and while one of us props him up, the other can paddle the dugout across the river to where the *Paloma* is moored. It's a long shot, but it's probably our only hope."

Manolo looked dubious. "Easy to make monkeys make noise," he said. He studied the Motilons who were paddling up and down the river. "But maybe eagle-eye Motilons see us as we cross over."

Tom nodded, lost in thought. "I know, Manolo. But I think we could sneak through them if we maneuver properly." He peered through the bushes. "There is plenty of open space between them."

He pulled out his knife and quickly cut through a shrub. A moment later he had a crude club about ten feet long. The Motilon, skirting the shore, as were some of the other Indians, was only twenty or thirty yards away now.

Tom drew in his breath sharply. "Okay, Manolo. This is it. Get those monkeys up there yammering and I'll swat this Motilon as he cruises by. And be ready to hop aboard the dugout quick. If he slumps over, it may capsize."

Manolo exchanged another glance with Tom and nodded. He picked up a stone and let fly. It caught one of the preacher monkeys in the pit of the stomach.

Tom waited tensely. The three monkeys were scampering from bough to bough, making an angry roar as they moved. None of the Motilons, he noticed, paid any particular attention. They were used to preacher monkeys and other jungle sounds, he told himself. Tom pushed through the underbrush and waited behind a clump of bushes on the river's edge. Ten yards, and now five. Just another second and—

Tom swung the club with every ounce of strength he had. It caught the Motilon on the side of his head, and the canoe swerved slightly as he slumped back from the blow. Before he could turn to look for Manolo, Tom saw him slip into the water and recover the paddle that had dropped from the Motilon's hands. Everything was working perfectly. The preacher monkeys were screaming their fury, and there was no dugout within forty yards. If it only would rain—but that would be too much to ask.

Tom reached out for the dugout canoe which Manolo was pushing toward him as he swam. A

moment later, Tom was crouched behind the Motilon, holding him up in a sitting position as Manolo,
concealing himself as much as possible, started paddling toward the opposite shore.

"Head to the left around that canoe over there,
and then make a beeline for the inlet the big dugout
just passed," Tom whispered.

CHAPTER EIGHTEEN

A MOTILON'S CUNNING

In spite of his awkward position, Manolo was able to paddle the canoe. Tom wondered what would happen if one of the other Motilons in a dugout started talking to this unconscious one. But he remembered that they seldom talked. Thank goodness they were so unsociable.

Tom's spirits were rising as they glided smoothly along. Out of the corner of his eye he could see the Motilons scanning the shore, looking for their prey. A gust of wind brought a suffocating odor toward them. Tom glanced at the shore and saw smoke rising from several scattered points not very far behind the spot they had vacated. It was obvious that the Motilons were making an all-out drive against them. They were trying to smoke them out with smudge fires, but it was too late for that now.

"Swerve to the left, Manolo," he whispered. "Keep as far from that big canoe as you can." This was the battleship in the Motilon fleet, Tom thought. And there were twenty-two eyes watching for some sign of them. The other dugout had disappeared from view.

229

Tom felt the Motilon he was propping up stir slightly. "Hurry, hurry, Manolo," he whispered. It was a race against time. A race against death. They were yards from the nearest dugout canoe now, and only about thirty yards from the inlet where he had moored the *Paloma*. He wondered whether the Blue Devil was on the *Paloma*. The Indians surely must have discovered it by now, but he wasn't worried so much about them. They wouldn't know how to operate a Diesel-driven launch. But the Blue Devil was not an ordinary Motilon.

Tom felt the cold perspiration breaking out on his brow. The Motilon he was holding was coming to. He leaned around him and saw that his eyelids were fluttering. There was only one thing to do now. Tom whipped out his bowie knife and pressed the point against the Indian's spine. That was a language even a Motilon would understand. He could feel the Indian stiffen. They were almost around the inlet now. Tom sat up then in the stern of the dugout so he would have more room for action.

"Pull in around this bend, Manolo," he whispered. He paused. He could hear Ozzy whimpering. He glanced back over his shoulder at the dugout canoes that were gliding up, down, and across the river. There was still a blockade to run, and he still had plenty of problems on his hands. Any second now this Motilon might swing into action. Tom had no idea what he'd do if the Indian tried to break free. Somehow, even to protect his own and Manolo's life, he could not bring himself to the thought of killing this savage foe.

"Okay, Manolo. They can't see us now. Let's head for the *Paloma*. Just ahead of us now—"

Tom turned his head at the sound of a voice speaking a loud dialect he couldn't understand. There, just a few yards away on the stern of the *Paloma*, was the Blue Devil, aiming an arrow directly at their dugout. The Motilon Tom had been guarding lurched back as he kicked at Manolo. A moment later Tom found himself in the water as the canoe overturned. He rose to the surface with a feeling of horror. He remembered how piranhas were attracted by the scent of blood, and he knew his knife had slightly pierced the skin of the Motilon's back. The Motilon was heading for him now. Manolo had not yet bobbed to the surface.

Tom slipped his knapsack off and swam toward the boat as an arrow whizzed by his ear. Out of the corner of his eye he saw Manolo swimming in the same direction. He heard the agonized scream of the Motilon who had upset the dugout, saw him flail around in the water for a brief second before he disappeared. There was only one thing that could make a Motilon scream with terror, he told himself. Piranhas! Tom shuddered.

"Go around the bow, Manolo. I'll try to climb aboard on this side while you do." Tom knew without glancing back that some of the Motilons near by must have heard the wails of the Motilon who had just gone under. But there was no time to look now. The whole thing was hopeless.

He wondered why the Blue Devil had not sent a shower of arrows at him and Manolo, but he could see why now. Ozzy, as if aware of his intention to kill Tom and Manolo, had leaped up and was clawing the Indian as he clung with his teeth to his right arm. As Tom cautiously pulled himself over the side and stepped over the rail he watched the Blue Devil's desperate attempt to pull Ozzy off.

Without a moment's hesitation Tom dove through the air and tackled the Motilon from the rear. He went down with a crash as Ozzy fell clear and growled as he sank his teeth in the savage's leg.

Tom turned, panting, to Manolo who was clambering aboard on the portside. "Quick, Manolo, go below and get a rope so we can tie this fellow up," he said. He pounced on the Blue Devil's back as he spoke and got a half nelson lock on him. He held on grimly. "Hurry, hurry, Manolo," he whispered. He was so physically and mentally exhausted he knew he couldn't hold onto the writhing Indian very long.

A moment later Manolo was winding the rope expertly around the Blue Devil's legs.

"Mr. Jason sound asleep below," he panted. "Again drugged."

"Thank . . . God. . . ." Tom felt like cheering. It was the best news he had had for so long. "Down, Ozzy, down," he ordered. "This smooth operator will give us no more trouble."

The Blue Devil, weakened by the ocelot's furious attack, and now securely bound, kept his eyes closed. Was the Indian planning something? Tom again examined the bonds. Yes, they were tight and, as far as he could see, the Indian could not possibly unfasten them.

Manolo drew Tom's attention from the Indian to the river.

"Tom, look!" Manolo said quietly. "Motilons come again."

As Tom looked he saw that the single canoes were appearing again from all the coves and along the shore. Those nearest the motorboat had quickly passed along the word that the search was ended. The quarry had been found. It was time for the kill. Tom took in the action on the river as he revved up the motor. It looked as if the Motilons were concentrating for an all-out assault. It was a matter of seconds before they would be greeted with a shower of arrows.

As the bow of the *Paloma* swung around, Tom

crouched low over the wheel. Then he left the wheel as the launch nosed out into the secret river. "Help me lift this guy up on this chair, Manolo. If the Motilons see him they may not shoot."

There was wild whooping among the Indians, whose canoes were arranged in formation as they closed in on the *Paloma*. Tom nudged the Blue Devil. "Order your men off or we'll feed you to the piranhas."

The Blue Devil's lips curled. "For more than fifteen years now, white explorers, adventurers, and missionaries have come into my domain. Not one has left to tell the story. And you will be no exception." He squirmed angrily in his chair and glared at Tom through narrowed eyes. "Unless," he said slowly, "you untie me and let me go."

Tom shook his head as he maneuvered the wheel. His glance shifted from the Blue Devil's face to the whooping Indians, who were trying to draw a bead on him. It was clear that the only reason they held back was through fear of hitting their chief.

"You're coming back to Belem with us, Mr. Blue Devil," he said. "You will be turned over to the Brazilian police. And I imagine they will have a lot of questions to ask you."

"Brave words," the Blue Devil sneered. "One command from me and my tribe will fill the air with arrows." His expression was grim and forbidding.

"You Will Die!" the Blue Devil Snarled

"You may as well learn now, young man, that I, like all my tribe, prefer death to captivity." His smile was mirthless. "I know how anxious the Brazilian government is to meet me."

Tom glared back at him. "Go below, Manolo, and bring up some of that nice raw hamburger that's in the freezer."

The Blue Devil glanced at him suspiciously. "None of your tricks will do you any good," he said.

Tom ignored him. "Bring enough," he called to Manolo, "to rub all over this Indian chief."

The Blue Devil blinked. "And just what do you expect to gain from all that?" he asked.

"It's just a little idea I had in case you get too frisky," Tom said, looking straight into his eyes. "One false move from you and we'll throw you over the side. And you know as well as I what will happen when the piranhas get a whiff of that raw hamburger."

"Very clever." The Blue Devil appeared to be pondering his course of action. Then he nodded and sighed. "Very well, young man. You win. Forget all about the hamburger and I'll call my men off."

"It's a deal. But be quick about it."

The Blue Devil turned in the direction of the Motilons and issued a command that Tom could not understand.

Tom glanced at Manolo, who had a troubled look.

He saw the look of blank amazement on the Motilons as they lowered their bows. Their dugouts turned and headed in the general direction of the pier.

"What's on your mind, Manolo?" Tom asked. "As far as I can see, things are turning out perfectly."

Manolo gestured toward the Blue Devil, who, eyes closed, had slumped back against his chair. "Blue Devil cannot be trusted," he said. "Plans trap."

The Blue Devil opened his eyes and strained angrily at his bonds. Hate shone in his bronze face for one fleeting second. Then, once again, he was the cool Indian chief.

Tom frowned. He rested his troubled gaze on the retreating Motilon fleet. "What makes you say that, Manolo?"

The little Indian shrugged. "Real Motilon dies before he surrender. Blue Devil surrender too easy. He is real Motilon." He shrugged again. "Must plan trap."

Tom thought fast. With the Indian fleet of dugouts behind them, it didn't seem possible that— "Hey, wait a minute." He nudged the Blue Devil again. "Where is that other big canoe with the eleven Motilons in it? I saw it head downstream quite a while ago."

Tom's eyes widened when he saw the mingled surprise and dark, concentrated fury on the Blue

Devil's face. That expression on his face told him all he wanted to know. Somewhere, thanks to the Blue Devil's cunning, a dugout canoe with eleven armed Motilons was waiting to ambush them.

CHAPTER NINETEEN

MAGIC COMMAND

Tom paced the deck nervously as Manolo took the wheel. He tested the Blue Devil's bonds to make sure they were still secure. He and Manolo and Uncle Leo had been through a lot during the past few days. And now, just when he thought they were past all danger, they were heading for the trap that the Blue Devil had planned.

Tom went below and leaned over his uncle, who was still lost to the world. He wished there was some way he could revive him. This was one of those times when he needed the missionary's wise counsel. Tom sank onto the opposite bunk and rested his face in his hands. He hadn't eaten all day, but he had no appetite. He was too excited to think of eating until they were out of the secret tunnel and back on the broad Amazon. It would be so wonderful to be back on the—

Tom jumped to his feet. Why hadn't he thought of it before! That secret tunnel. The only exit from the Blue Devil's hidden kingdom. A dark, narrow passage—a perfect place for an ambush! So that was it! That's where the big dugout must be waiting.

Tom rubbed his chin and nodded to himself. The Blue Devil thought of everything.

What could he and Manolo do to outwit this clever fellow? True they had him in bonds, but what good would that do them when they reached the secret river? It would not be long before some of the Motilon warriors would board the *Paloma* and set free their leader. And, as far as Tom knew, there was no other way out to the Amazon except through the tunnel-like passageway that they had gone through when entering the Motilon territory.

Tom paced the deck looking, searching for some way to outwit the Blue Devil—some way to thwart his plans of an ambush. Perhaps, he thought, they might have something that the leader would like to own. If he could only think of what it might be, perhaps he could trade that article for their safe passage. But think as hard as he could, he could find nothing. The small trinkets Mr. Jason used to trade with other tribes meant nothing to this fellow.

Tom's glance slowly shifted to the recording machine his uncle always took with him on the *Paloma,* so he could record the dialects of the Indians he served. A simple but effective plan was forming in his mind. He remembered the short command the Blue Devil had given the Motilons. Their bows had immediately dropped. They had, without hesitation, turned and headed back toward the pier. If he could record that command it would be a cinch. Just play the machine as they cruised through the tunnel and the Motilons would recognize their master's voice. It was that simple.

Tom went topside and blindfolded the Blue Devil so he couldn't see what was going on. Then he went below again and returned a moment later with the recording machine. He sat down near the Blue Devil, holding it in his lap, ready to switch it on at the right moment.

"You know, Mr. Blue Devil, you really had us worried for a few minutes," he said. "Manolo and I really thought you were leading us into an ambush of some kind." He saw that not a muscle in the Indian's face twitched. "Then I realized that you were a little different from your savage tribe. You have had a different kind of life, and life means more to you than to them, am I right?"

"I'm so glad you understand," the Blue Devil said softly. "My tribe and I are different, naturally. Our values are different." He forced a smile. "So it shouldn't seem too surprising that I find death less attractive than they."

Tom leaned forward. "Yet they obey your every word, Mr. Blue Devil. One word from you works wonders." He tried to sound casual. "For example, look how they obeyed your command a while back. Just what was it you said, by the way?" Tom quickly turned on the switch of the recorder.

"*Lonna walla tanganika,*" the Blue Devil said. Tom switched off the recorder. "It means 'return to your quarters at once.' "

Tom nodded. For once the Blue Devil was telling the truth. For this was the exact command he had given a few minutes before.

He looked up to find Manolo smiling at him. "Mr. Jason awake now," he said.

Tom leaped to his feet. "Wow! Now we're cooking on all four burners," he shouted.

"Three." Manolo smiled. "Mr. Jason. You. Me."

Tom patted him on the back affectionately. "You sure are picking up American slang, Manolo. I'll be right back. I want to go below and see how Uncle Leo is feeling."

The missionary listened to all that had happened since he had last seen Tom. He beamed when Tom explained how he had tricked the Blue Devil into dictating the magic command into the recording machine.

He sat up on his bunk and extended his hand. "Tom, I just want to say now that I am more than just proud of you. It's been a miracle that we have been able to live through the past few days in this jungle."

"We sure have been lucky." Tom lay down and propped his head against a pillow. "I guess I know

Tom Switched on the Recorder

what happened to you. When you reached the top of the cliff the Blue Devil was there waiting, right, Uncle Leo?"

"Right. All I can remember, really, is a struggle and being hit with something. But that's all behind us now." He rubbed his chin thoughtfully. "One more obstacle to pass and we're out of this mess. Our first job is to gag the Blue Devil to keep him from issuing any countercommand."

Tom nodded as he headed up the ladder. "I thought of that myself." He glanced at his watch. "Ten minutes before one. We should reach the tunnel in less than half an hour."

Tom and Manolo carried the Blue Devil below and put him in a bunk, while the missionary took the wheel. Then Tom adjusted the volume of the recording machine and made sure that everything was ready.

Scarcely another word was spoken as the *Paloma* churned its way toward the secret tunnel where, if their suspicions were correct, the eleven Motilons would be waiting to ambush them. Tom looked up into the cloudless blue sky and yawned. It reminded him of the day they had cruised into the other end of the secret tunnel. But what adventures he had had since that day!

He had exchanged glances with the missionary and Manolo as he rested the recorder in his lap.

"This is it," their nods meant. Tom wet his lips and strained to listen as the prow of the *Paloma* nosed into the dark, narrow passage. In a moment they would know their fate.

CHAPTER TWENTY

HOMEWARD CRUISE

For what seemed an eternity to Tom the *Paloma* swished its way through the calm waters of the secret river. Except for the throbbing of the launch's motor, there was complete silence. Tom probed the dim-lit winding passage, searching for the first sign of the dugout containing the Motilons. He could see nothing. Perhaps their suspicions had been ill-founded. Maybe the big dugout had returned while they were not looking.

They hardly dared to breathe. The jungle, too, seemed to be keeping their silence. Not a leaf moved. The trees overhanging the channel were motionless. Even the preacher monkeys that usually chattered incessantly were still. The churning of the water put in motion by the boat and the soft lapping of the waves against the shore were the only sounds. The stillness was ominous.

Tom, with Manolo beside him, looked ahead searching everywhere along the stream. Where could the dugout be? It was certainly impossible that it could have passed the *Paloma* and not one of them had seen it. It also seemed unlikely that there was another secret passage, for the whole stream was lined with shrubs and trees. The canoe *must* be ahead of them.

The missionary's whisper broke the silence. "If I remember right, there is a nice secluded spot about fifty yards beyond the next curve. As we round the curve, Tom, flash a beam of light and see if you can spot anything. If those Indians are hiding there, they'll know we're coming anyway, so the light won't make any difference as far as that's concerned."

"Righto, Uncle."

Tom held his breath as the *Paloma* slowly swung around the bend. Suddenly the missionary revved the motor and the launch sped forward faster. And then it happened. In the beam of light Tom saw the dugout gliding slowly almost against the edge of the passage, mostly hidden by the overhanging branches. As the *Paloma* churned toward the ambush, an arrow whizzed past the missionary's head. Tom turned on the switch as a second arrow missed him by inches as he flopped onto the deck.

"*Lonna walla tanganika.*" Tom turned the instrument off and wound it back. He had it ready again just as the *Paloma* sped past the bewildered Indians. "*Lonna walla tanganika.*"

From his crouching position Tom could see the look of wild amazement in the expressions of the Indians. It was plain as day that they didn't understand the order. Tom waited until they started rowing back toward their private kingdom before he sat up.

He grinned at his uncle. "Well, Uncle Leo, we didn't run into Colonel Fawcett. We didn't find any trace of the lost mountain city. In fact, we didn't even find an oil well." He glanced affectionately at Manolo, whose wan face was lit up with a smile. "But I wouldn't say it was exactly boring, would you, Manolo?"

"Only sometimes," Manolo said. "And those times I like best."

The missionary's eyes filled with a dreamy look. "Well, boys, it's still early in the summer. After we get our friend, the Blue Devil, straightened out, maybe we'll solve, once and for all, the riddle of the Motilons."

Tom drummed on the railing. He saw the broad expanse of the mighty Amazon as the *Paloma* swung past the entrance of the secret river and headed for Belem.

He rose and stretched. "I think I'll go below and have a little chat with the Blue Devil," he said. "Maybe I can persuade him to tell me more about those oil wells."

OTHER ADVENTURES
of
TOM STETSON

"Tom Stetson and the Blue Devil," is the third of the fascinating adventures of Tom, his uncle, and the Indian boy, Manolo. In all of the books, the author, John Henry Cutler, weaves into the Amazon jungle background, exciting tales of tense mystery and adventure.

Tom Stetson and the Giant Jungle Ants

Tom Stetson watches a thin column of smoke rise above the Brazilian jungle. It can mean but one thing —an Indian village is there. But no Indian village is supposed to be there! Tom has been with his uncle, Leo Jason, only a week, but already his promise of adventure is coming true.

On the jungle trail that Tom, his uncle, and the young Indian boy, Manolo, follow, they find new excitement and dangers. A column of giant jungle ants devouring everything in its path, an Indian captive guarded by four ferocious eagles, a native village where young men must undergo unheard-of tests of endurance to prove their manhood, are but a few of the sights and experiences that fill Tom's days.

When Manolo is captured by a savage tribe, Tom and Uncle Leo find themselves in real difficulty. Without weapons, they must outwit the tribe and rescue their young friend. Only one way suggests itself, a way so daring that Uncle Leo can scarcely believe it possible. How this plan is carried out against many odds, makes a grim and exciting climax to this tale of adventure in the Brazilian jungle.

Tom Stetson on the Trail of the Lost Tribe

While searching the jungle for their lost Indian friend, Manolo, Tom Stetson and his uncle, Leo Jason, encounter strange and exciting adventures. At one time they are trapped between a wall of flame and a savage Indian tribe; and again they are chased by savages along a treetop cable.

Their search carries them deep into the jungle where few white men have gone before. Tom finds the customs of the natives interesting and he observes the Indians closely while he and his uncle are detained in their camp. He is taken on a fishing trip unlike any he has ever heard of; he learns about the natives' weird tribal ceremonies as he watches breathlessly while thousands of brilliant butterflies are released from the sun temple, and he looks on while an enemy spy is tortured by the dread alligator fly. All the color, beauty, and savagery of the great Amazon wilderness forms the setting for a story of mystery and thrilling adventure.

WHITMAN BOOKS
FOR BOYS AND GIRLS

NEW STORIES
OF ADVENTURE AND MYSTERY

Up-to-the-minute novels for boys and girls about favorite characters, all popular and well known—

ROY ROGERS and the Rimrod Renegades
ROY ROGERS and the Outlaws of Sundown Valley
ROY ROGERS and the Ghost of Mystery Rancho
ROY ROGERS and the Gopher Creek Gunman
ROY ROGERS and the Raiders of Sawtooth Ridge

GENE AUTRY and the Big Valley Grab
GENE AUTRY and the Badmen of Broken Bow
GENE AUTRY and the Golden Ladder Gang
GENE AUTRY and the Thief River Outlaws
GENE AUTRY and the Redwood Pirates

THE BOBBSEY TWINS: Merry Days Indoors and Out
THE BOBBSEY TWINS in the Country
THE BOBBSEY TWINS at the Seashore

WHITMAN BOOKS
FOR BOYS AND GIRLS

NEW STORIES
OF ADVENTURE AND MYSTERY

THE WALTON BOYS in High Country
THE WALTON BOYS in Rapids Ahead
THE WALTON BOYS and Gold in the Snow

SAND DUNE PONY

TOM STETSON and the Blue Devil
TOM STETSON and the Giant Jungle Ants
TOM STETSON on the Trail of the Lost Tribe

GINNY GORDON and the Mystery at the Old Barn
GINNY GORDON and the Mystery of the Missing Heirloom
GINNY GORDON and the Disappearing Candlesticks

TRIXIE BELDEN and the Gatehouse Mystery
TRIXIE BELDEN and the Red Trailer Mystery
TRIXIE BELDEN and the Secret of the Mansion

The books listed above may be purchased at
the same store where you secured this book.